W9-AOI-396

DEFIANCE

DEFIANCE

VALERIE HOBBS

SQUARE
FISH

FARRAR, STRAUS AND GIROUX

NEW YORK

"Should There Be a Day" is reprinted with permission from Julia Cunningham.

SQUARE FISH

An Imprint of Macmillan

DEFIANCE. Copyright © 2005 by Valerie Hobbs. All rights reserved. Printed in April 2009 in the United States of America by R.R. Donnelley & Sons Company, Harrisonburg, Virginia. For information, address Square Fish, 175 Fifth Avenue, New York, NY 10010.

Square Fish and the Square Fish logo are trademarks of Macmillan and are used by Farrar, Straus and Giroux under license from Macmillan.

Library of Congress Cataloging-in-Publication Data
Hobbs, Valerie.
    Defiance / Valerie Hobbs.
        p.   cm.
    Summary: While vacationing in the country, eleven-year-old Toby, a cancer patient, learns some important lessons about living and dying from an elderly poet and her cow.
    ISBN: 978-0-312-53581-0
    [1. Death—Fiction.   2. Hope—Fiction.   3. Cancer—Fiction.
4. Poets—Fiction.   5. Cows—Fiction.   6. Country life—Fiction.]
I. Title.

PZ7.H65237 De 2005
[Fic]—dc22

                                            2004061524

Originally published in the United States by Farrar, Straus and Giroux
Square Fish logo designed by Filomena Tuosto
Book design by Barbara Grzeslo
First Square Fish Edition: 2009
10 9 8 7 6 5 4
www.squarefishbooks.com

To Julia Cunningham

SHOULD THERE BE A DAY

Should there be a day
when you are not
and I am yet with breath
what shall I say
what shall I ask of death?
Come get the rest
the half of me that stays
shallow of heart, hollow as a bone?
Or shall I determine to forget
delight entombed, alone,
follow the foggy way
of self-deceit and let
the sun of truth go out?
I do not know. I must pass
the answer by. But if one tree
allows itself to rise,
one spear of grass to spike,
one rose to show its core
then surely what of me is you
must grow beyond your night
keep faith with what you were
and, more, be constant, whole and move
within the light that was your gift of love.

—Julia Cunningham

DEFIANCE

Toby knew he was in trouble, but the cow didn't. She just kept gazing at him with her huge brown eyes, like she was in love or something. So he went on petting her, even though he wasn't supposed to be here. His mother would have a fit if she knew. She was always having a fit about something, even out here in the country, where they were supposed to be having a vacation.

The cow was really big, and at first, when he'd stopped his bicycle to get a closer look, Toby was a little bit afraid of her. Didn't even know it was a "her" until he saw what was underneath, her huge pink udder swollen with milk. It made him think about the time at the hospital when he was just a little kid, eight or nine. How his eyes kept sliding over to the box of doctor gloves by the side of the sink. He knew very well that he wasn't supposed to touch anything, but they'd left him alone in the examining room for such a long time.

That was when Toby understood for the first time what being sick really meant. Nobody had yelled at him, not even when the glove full of water slipped from his hand and spurted out all over the room, all over the nurse who always saved him the grape Tootsie Pops. Nobody said a word. Sick kids got away with stuff.

Like this morning. When he got back to the cabin, his mother would probably threaten to ground him. Or make him return the bicycle to the shed where he'd found it. But her threats were mostly hot air. All Toby had to do was act tired or touch his side. "Are you okay, honey?" she'd say, smoothing her hand over his head. "Are you feeling all right?"

The cow's head was ten times bigger than a person's, and hanging over the fence as if she had been waiting for somebody just like Toby to come along and pet her. Somebody who didn't mind the fat blue flies that buzzed around her eyes and ears. And now she wouldn't let him go. If he tried to take his hand away, she'd bump it with her nose and make him start all over again.

It was a warm morning, growing hotter as the sun climbed the sky. Toby could feel it on his back and on the back of his neck. Sweat trickled from under his Giants cap and down the sides of his face. He let it be. The flies buzzed in circles around the cow's head, and somewhere in the distance a tractor coughed and started. The world was waking up. The cow stayed right where she was. So did Toby. Inside, there was this peaceful feeling. As if he'd never have to do another thing forever but stand here and pet this big old black-and-white cow.

Big, but skinny. Skinnier than cows were supposed to be, at least the ones he saw on TV or in books. You could see where her ribs were trying to poke through. Cows ate grass, that was one thing he knew, and this cow was standing in a whole field full. Grass and weeds and purple flowers that he thought might be clover. So why was she so skinny? Where did she live anyway? Where did she sleep? Not a barn in sight. But he'd passed a dirt driveway that had a banged-up mailbox at the end of it. Whoever didn't love this cow enough probably lived down that driveway.

He wondered what the cow was thinking about him. He was skinny, too. Tall for eleven, but she probably wouldn't know that. Maybe she was wondering about the bruises on his arms. It was hard to tell with cows.

Tomorrow he'd bring her an apple, or some Cheerios.

But today, right now, he had to get home. He gave the cow one last rub between the eyes. It was still early. If his mother wasn't up yet, he could sneak the bike back into the shed.

Using the fence post for support, Toby climbed back onto the bike. Like a girl, lifting his right leg over the bar. He wished he were strong enough to leap up and land on the seat, the right way, the way the boys at school did. But at least he had a bike to ride. Pushing off with his left foot, Toby wobbled toward home.

The road stretched ahead of him into the distance. Longer than when he was coming down it, though that couldn't be. After a while, he stopped the bike, sweat running down his face, dripping from his chin. He took off his cap, pulled up his T-shirt, and wiped his whole head with it. He began to walk the bike. It was easy in the shade, but harder as the road began to climb.

It seemed to go on forever, snaking up through dappled shade. Toby watched his feet instead of the road, one sneakered foot going forward, then the other, fooling himself into thinking it wasn't so steep, or so far. All the same, he was out of breath by the time he got to the top. So beat, he thought about leaving the bike at the foot of the drive that led to their rented cabin.

But the only way to keep it for tomorrow, and all the tomorrows after that, was to hide the old bike in the shed. He bent himself into one last push, breathing hard, leaning into the worn rubber handle grips for support. And when he lifted his head, there was his mother. She was standing on the porch in her fuzzy blue bathrobe with her fists on her hips and her black curls poking out of her head like springs.

"Toby?"

Head down, Toby pushed the bike across the dry grass and laid it against the side of the cabin. It didn't have a kickstand. It didn't even have a front fender. But at least it was a bike. In the city he wasn't allowed to ride a bike. He still wasn't very good at it.

"Toby? What did I tell you, young man?"

She was eight feet tall from where he stood at the base of the steps. "You mean, about the bike?"

"You know very well what I mean. Did I *not* say you were *not* to ride the bicycle until we could get you a helmet? Did you *not* hear me say that? Toby?" He hated the way her eyebrows pinched together in the middle when she was angry.

Once, when she'd been yelling at him just like this, a bubble of laughter had started up in his belly. Because her eyebrows looked exactly like two fighting caterpillars. He'd tried his hardest to swallow down the bubble, but it tickled right up his throat and jumped out. And then he just couldn't stop. He laughed so hard he lost his breath and had to roll on the floor clutching his stomach. Which only made things worse. So now he had to not think about caterpillars, which only made him think about caterpillars.

"Yeah," he said.

Her face came down over him, pinched and white-looking. "Pardon me?"

"I mean yes. Yes, *Mother*. I heard you."

"Oh, Toby," she said, sighing her sad sigh. She frowned at him for a while without saying anything at all, her arms crossed. Then she gathered her robe around her legs and sat down on the top step, where her face was even with his. "Don't you get it, honey?" she said. "You've got to take better care of yourself. I can't be watching you all the time."

"I do take good care of myself."

"You didn't take the cell phone."

"I forgot."

"What about sunscreen? Did you at least put on sunscreen?"

Toby lied to his mother sometimes, more and more lately. It was the only way he could get her to leave him alone. But it always made him feel bad. Only weenies and bad people told lies, or so he thought before he began to tell them.

"Yup," he said, and swallowed hard.

"The number thirty?"

"Uh huh."

"All over?"

"All over."

One of her caterpillar eyebrows arched its back. "Then you must have sweated it all off because I can't smell it."

This was when he could have said, "Right! I sweated it off," or told her it was the *unscented* stuff. But the best liars knew when to keep their mouths shut. And they looked their mothers straight in the eye without flinching. Trouble was, their mothers didn't flinch either.

It seemed like forever before his mother finally stood up and said, "Come on inside. I'm making crepes."

The kitchen wasn't much of a kitchen. It didn't have a real stove for one thing. But he'd watched his mother make a ham and cheese omelet over a campfire once and knew she could cook anything, even on the little stove thing, which was just two burners that got plugged into the wall.

Butter sizzled in the frying pan. His mother tipped in the crepe batter so that it covered the bottom of the pan like a thin sheet of plastic. "Daddy called," she said. "He might not be able to make it tomorrow."

"Again?" Toby's father was supposed to drive up on

Friday nights and stay the weekend. That was the plan. His father would come and they would do stuff, hike, go out on the lake. Toby would learn how to fish. But in the three weeks he and his mother had stayed in the cabin, his father had come only once. He was "knocked out," he'd said, and slept in the hammock all Saturday afternoon. Toby's mother stuck tiny tomato plants into a patch of dug-up ground. Then she got up, dusted off her knees, and went inside to practice her cello. Toby sat on the porch reading *Holes* to the somber drone of Mozart. He would have been out riding the bike, but his father had forgotten to bring him a helmet. He felt like a prisoner, like Stanley Yelnats at Camp Green Lake.

Except that there really was a lake, and it was green. Sort of furry along the sides. Algae, his father said it was. Bacteria, his mother said. And that was the end of any ideas about swimming.

Toby smeared his crepe with strawberry jam, ate a couple of bites. Then a couple more because it was easier to chew and swallow than listen to a lecture.

"Don't forget your pills," his mother said, like she always said. A zillion tablets and capsules and vitamins. Red ones, green ones, yellow ones, round ones, ones too big to swallow that had to be chopped in half, capsules with powder inside or oily liquid, big ugly brown pills that smelled like barf. One half cup. It said so right there on the plastic measuring cup his mother put them in. "We don't need you to get sick."

I'm already sick, he could have said, but didn't. It wasn't something they talked about. It was something they did. He and his mother and his father, the way other families got ready for Disneyland or Hawaii, only different. No laughing or looking forward to. There really wasn't any way to get ready for being sick. You just did it. Packed your clothes and books, your laptop. Tried not to think about the surgery and all the chemo that would come after. Three months at Children's Hospital, where other kids like him got better or worse or just disappeared, their beds made up as if they'd never been there. Toby didn't want to think about his time there now that it was over.

Only it wasn't. On the third morning after they'd settled into the cabin, Toby had felt it again. It was in the same spot on his right side, a slippery marble. He'd jumped out of bed and hurried into his clothes, covering it up.

His mom had been standing at the little kitchen sink sipping her coffee. There were purple shadows under her eyes. "Sleep all right, honey?"

"Sure."

She looked out the window. "It's going to be hot today. Did you pack your trunks?"

"My trunks?" *Was he hearing right? The lake was off-limits, wasn't it?*

"I thought you could help me for a while in the garden," she said. "Then we could . . . Oh, I don't know . . ." Her smile was lopsided, as if she was out of practice. "Run through the sprinkler to cool off! Or are you too old for that?"

"I'm eleven, Mom," he said. "Jeez!" *Run through the sprinkler? Was she nuts?* And anyway, he did have his trunks. He just couldn't wear them. Or she would see. Her eagle eyes would go straight to the marble and he would be back at Children's Hospital in no time flat. She would call an ambulance. Or get a helicopter. Only he wasn't going to do all that again. He wasn't going to puke up his guts over and over while his mother held his head. He wasn't going to miss school and lose what few friends he had left. He wasn't going to make new friends with kids who disappeared. It would be the biggest lie he'd ever told, and he would tell it over and over again whenever she asked him how he was, no matter how bad it made him feel.

"Fine," he'd tell her. "I'm fine."

The next morning, Toby was up before the sun. Dressed in yesterday's clothes, he carried his sneakers down the hall, past the room where his mother slept. In the kitchen, he filled both his pockets with Cheerios. Then he crossed to the screen door, opening it inch by inch so that it wouldn't screech.

Moths circled the porch light. With one hand still on the door, Toby looked out at the lake. It was covered in a thick gray mist, cattails poking through along the edge. Pretty, but kind of creepy, too. If he waited maybe two seconds, some horrible thing, all claws and dripping teeth, would come rearing up out of the water. There! Right out *there*!

Too many movies. His mother was probably right, though he'd never tell her that.

He left the porch and crossed the wet grass, trying to ignore the cold hand of air that kept reaching for his neck. Imagination, that was all it was. The trick was to keep one step ahead of it.

The bike was leaning where he'd left it against the side of the cabin. It was wet with dew, gleaming in the predawn light as if overnight it had lost all its rust and dents. Toby pushed it all the way down the drive and out onto the road. Then, with his heart knocking hard, he stood with the bike between his legs and looked down into the pool of darkness at the bottom of the hill. Before he could chicken out, he lifted his right foot and pushed off.

Sailing down the hill into the pitch-black dark, Toby clung to the wet handle grips, too scared to whoop, even to breathe. Then suddenly he was on flat ground, coasting fast. Way off on the horizon a strip of brightness opened. Then, like a balloon someone had let go, the sun began to rise. Sunlight glinted in the fields on both sides. In one field a huge bull stood absolutely still, like something cut out of black paper. In the next, two horses leaned against each other, head to rump. Were they sleeping? Holding each other up?

There was so much he didn't know. Everything he knew came out of books or off the Internet. This was different, real life.

The cow was standing in the same place, her head hanging over the fence. He reached into his pockets and offered her the Cheerios. She slurped them out of his cupped hands with a single swipe of her big slick tongue. Toby wished he'd brought more, the whole box. But even that wouldn't have been enough. He stood on the side of the road for a long time petting her, and the longer he stood, the angrier he got. How could the man who owned such a nice cow let her starve to death?

Farther down the road was the dirt driveway he'd passed the day before, the one with the dented mailbox. A city kid, he knew better than to talk to strangers. Still, somebody had to help this cow. He got on the bike and coasted down the road standing up.

The driveway had deep ruts all along it. Toby got off his bike, pushing it ahead of him. The field on his left had rows and rows of corn plants so tall he could see only the clear blue sky above them. On his right the cow's field had nothing but weeds and clover. A small brown rabbit darted out of the weeds. Seeing Toby, it stopped dead. Toby stopped, too, but the rabbit darted back.

Quiet. Nothing but the sound of his sneakers slapping the hard dry earth. He was getting used to it, to the feeling of quiet. The first night in the cabin, he hadn't been able to sleep. But he liked the silence now. He liked being alone in the quiet morning, nobody to tell him where to go, what not to do. He liked making his own decisions for a change. The bike bumped along beside him like a friend willing to do any dumb thing he said.

The house seemed to rise up all at once out of the fields. It wasn't what he'd hoped for, a friendly-looking farmhouse with a wide front porch and a tire swing hanging from a tree. This house was beaten up, its roof caving toward the middle and missing lots of shingles. Closer, Toby could see the many colors the house had been over the years: gray, brown, blue. Paint wearing away until there was nothing left but bare boards. No porch. If there had ever been one, it was gone now. A flat rock had been laid for a step leading up to a faded blue door. The door had a sign on it Toby couldn't read from where he stood.

Starting at the road and stretching almost as far as the stone step was a vegetable garden. Tomatoes, corn with its silky hair still on, lettuce, purple cabbage, green beans strung on a line like Christmas lights. The garden made the house seem not so daunting.

He inched his bike closer, trying to make out what was written on the paper tacked to the door. The words were scrawled in crabby-looking handwriting. He was nearly to the step before he could read them all.

WHOEVER STEALS MY FREEDOM
TAKES MY LIFE

Toby read the sign twice, trying to decide what kind of person would write a thing like that. Was it somebody who would listen to what a boy had to say about a cow? While he was deciding what to do, a black-and-white-speckled chicken fluttered down from a tree and began pecking the ground. Then out of nowhere came an ear-shattering explosion. The chicken's head snapped up and it froze where it stood, but Toby was on his bike and out of there, bumping down the rutted road as fast as the bike would go.

Was it a gun? It sounded like a gun. But he'd never heard a live gun, only the ones in the movies or on TV. Pedaling as fast as his legs could manage, he turned his head only once and saw the farmhouse sinking slowly behind the field.

Pushing his bike up the driveway to the cabin, Toby hardly thought about his mother and how upset she would be. He was just glad to be home. Dizzy-tired, covered with sweat, he made it to the top of the drive.

And there was his father's car.

Toby stared at the little red cabin as if he could learn something from it. It was Friday, but his father wasn't supposed to be here. His mother had said his father wasn't coming for the weekend. Or did she say he *might* not come?

Whatever. The fact was that his father was here, and Toby was in for it now.

He laid the bike against the cabin and trudged toward the door. Through the screen he could hear his parents arguing. They were always arguing, sometimes about Toby, though he wasn't supposed to know that. He pulled open the door, making it shriek. His parents' heads turned. His mother frowned, but his father came toward him with a big smile. "Hey, guy!" Knowing what was coming, Toby got into his boxer's stance. His father crouched, fake-punched Toby on the arm. "Where have you been, guy?"

Toby shrugged. "Out riding."

"Hey, great!" Toby watched his father turn toward his mother as if to say, *See? He's all right. You're worried about nothing.*

"He doesn't have a helmet, David," Toby's mother said, tight-lipped.

"Well, he does now." His father reached into his pocket and tossed Toby the car keys. "It's in the trunk. Top of the line, wait till you see it. I brought your telescope from home, too."

"Thanks, Dad!" Toby escaped out the door.

The silver helmet had orange lightning bolts on both

sides. Toby stuck it on his head, letting the straps hang free. Then he lifted out his telescope, wrapped like a baby in a blanket. It had been an expensive one, top of the line his father said. Although he'd helped Toby set it up so that he could stargaze through his bedroom window, his father had never looked through it. Toby's mother did sometimes, if he could pull her away from whatever else she was doing. "Wow," she'd say, but he could tell she didn't get it, what it felt like to be part of a whole galaxy.

He took the telescope inside and set it up in his room. His father had gone out to lie in the hammock. "Rough week," he said. "I wish I could stay until Sunday, but work is work!"

He rallied after lunch. "Let's take the boat out," he said. "See if the old thing floats."

"Toby can't go in that water," his mother said.

"Will you *stop*?" his father said. "There's nothing wrong with Toby. He's perfectly all right. Look at him."

His mother looked at Toby, even though she saw him all the time and knew perfectly well what he looked like, a bald-headed boy with eyes too big for his long narrow face. The same boy the kids at school saw and shied away from, as if he had some highly infectious respiratory disease.

"Don't worry," his father said. "The boat's not going to sink. Worst comes to worst, we'll bail her out." He got up from the table and went to the door. "Come on! What are you waiting for? Get your suits on."

When Toby climbed into the boat wearing one of his father's T-shirts, his father didn't seem to notice. His mother got in like she was stepping into a bathtub with her flowered bathing suit on. Her straw hat looked like a flying saucer. She handed Toby the sunscreen. He smeared it over his arms and legs. "Don't forget your neck," she said.

"Take that shirt off, son," his father said. He already had a tan, or looked as if he did because of his dark skin. "Get some sun. The two of you are pale as fish."

Toby stared at his father, then he looked over at his mother, who was also staring at his father. *Get it over with,* said a voice inside, *get it over with. Take off your shirt and let them see it. Then tell them you're finished with it, finished with the whole dang thing, no matter what they say.*

He reached down to pull off his shirt.

3

Saturday morning Toby was pushing his bike once more on the rutted driveway to the farmhouse. Nothing could get him down today, not even the fact that the cow wasn't waiting at the fence. To think he could be having a CAT scan right this minute, hanging around the hospital while they decided what to do about him. Instead, he was free, and all because his mother had made him keep his shirt on. The sun was much too hot out on the lake, she'd said. And so his secret was safe.

He mounted the bike and drove straight through the ruts, taking the bumps in his stride.

Last night in an e-mail Toby had told his friend Pop-eye all about the cow and the broken-down farmhouse and, finally, the explosion. It was a great story, and he couldn't wait to hear back from her. She was the only kid from Children's Hospital who kept in touch, a girl who made fun of everything, even the way her cancer made her eye stick out.

And she was the bravest girl, the bravest *person*, he'd ever met. He'd never forget the time he and Popeye had sneaked out of the hospital, right under the noses of the staff. They didn't do much but walk around the grounds, but they talked about everything in the world. What they liked to read and eat and watch on TV. And, finally, about the thing that made them most alike, their illness. But even about that, she was brave. Not to worry, she said, not to worry. Popeye was the one person Toby could talk straight to, but he couldn't tell even her what he'd decided not to do.

Toby was nearly to the farmhouse when he heard the screeching. All at once he saw a clutch of crows lift into the sky and settle back down, exactly like the four and twenty blackbirds in the children's rhyme. He got off his bike. Crouching, he pushed it closer to the farmhouse.

What he saw then was enough to send him racing home again. A witch with white hair flying around her head was jabbing a crooked stick up into a tree, thick with leaves. "Scat! Scat! Thankless fiends! Ill-bred monsters!" The crows screamed back. A few flew circles above the tree, but the rest stayed within the leaves, cawing as if they'd come for a party and weren't about to leave. "Out! Villains! Marble-hearted fiends!" The witch circled the tree, one arm out to gauge her distance from it, the other poking with the stick. And then as Toby watched, bug-eyed, she fell forward with a cry, landing on her hands and knees.

Without thinking, Toby dropped his bike and ran to help her up. She was as light and dry as paper. "Are you okay?"

The witch looked at him through milky blue eyes. "Oh, yes, I'm quite all right. Who are you?" She reached her thin bumpy fingers toward his face. Toby shrank back, though he wasn't afraid. He didn't really believe in witches, and this one, even if she was one, was tinier than witches ought to be. And she wore overalls. He was pretty sure a real witch wouldn't be caught dead in bib overalls.

"Toby," he said.

"I didn't hear you come up the driveway," she said. She leaned toward him, her voice lowered to a whisper. "Are you alone?"

"Yes, ma'am," Toby said, then thought better of it. There was nobody around for miles, nobody to call for help if he needed it. In his mind was his mother's cell phone sitting on the kitchen table in the cabin.

"I am Pearl," the witch, who couldn't really be a witch, said. "Come inside, I need you to do something for me." She turned toward the house. He watched her walk away, the crooked stick thumping beside her. At the door, she stopped and turned. "Well, come on," she said. "I'm not going to bite you."

More curious than afraid, Toby followed the old woman into the house. The room she led him through was too filled with junk to be a living room, magazines and newspapers stacked in all the places there wasn't any furniture, and there was a lot of that. Big old dark stuff, a huge clock with Roman numerals, bookcases filled with dusty books and strung with cobwebs. What light there was came through pulled-down window shades, yellowish, dust floating through. A tattered green couch was piled high with still more magazines, and a grand piano, closed, was covered with books. On a shelf above the piano a plaster angel with fat cheeks and droopy wings gazed gloomily down on everything.

Pearl used her stick to get through the maze, knocking it into whatever lay ahead of her. She stopped beside a rocking chair that held a basket full of unopened mail. "There," she said, tapping her stick on the basket. "Get that."

When Toby picked up the basket, some of the envelopes fell to the floor. By the time he retrieved them, Pearl had thumped out of the room. He found her in the kitchen at the end of a dimly lit hallway. The kitchen was flooded with sunlight. In the middle was a small round table with a blue-checked tablecloth and four red chairs with backs like ladders. A gray cat lay in the center of the tablecloth licking her paw. "You can start by separating it," Pearl said. She pointed a shaky finger at him, or at the basket in his hands. "Bills and letters. If it even looks like a bill or one of those advertisements, toss it in the trash. Then you can read me the rest."

She was like a teacher. Toby felt like his six-year-old self waiting for Mrs. Edmunds to give him the pencils he was to hand out to each student. It was an important job, but he didn't know if he was up to it, or why, of all the kids, she had chosen him. It didn't occur to him, then or now, to turn the job down.

"Set it right there on the table. Get off, Geraldine." She nudged the cat, who held her ground until there wasn't any left, then dropped with a thump to the floor. "I'll make us some tea. You do drink tea, don't you?"

Toby didn't, but he said he did. The way she asked made him feel as if he had to. As if he were in danger of being uncivilized or—what had she called the crows?—thankless. He began sorting Pearl's mail, making the two piles she asked for, but not yet throwing any away. There was hardly anything but bills and advertisements, all addressed to Ms. Pearl Richardson or sometimes Pearl Rhodes Richardson. As he sorted, he watched her move around the kitchen, feeling for the knob on the cupboard where the teacups were, then lighting the stove with shaky fingers and a wooden match. On the wall behind the stove a huge black smudge went all the way up to the ceiling.

By the time Toby finished sorting the mail, there were only two letters not in the throwaway pile. He gathered up all the rest and dropped it into a trash can beside the back door.

The teacup Pearl set in front of Toby was tiny, with a fancy golden handle and flowers painted on it and on the saucer, too. The cup was hard to pick up because you couldn't stick your finger through the handle. The tea smelled and tasted just like straw.

"You're a very large-headed young man," Pearl said. "Is that an indication of the size of your brain, I wonder?"

Toby reached up and touched the helmet that was still on his head. "It's the helmet," he said. Then, because his manners weren't as bad as she probably thought, he took it off and set it on the table. It was a relief to know she couldn't see him well. He'd never quite gotten used to the way people's faces changed when they saw that he was bald. First surprise, then pity. Then they'd go blank, as if nothing was different at all.

"I don't see like I used to," Pearl said. "But I manage. Better than *some* people think I do. Why, if it were up to them, I'd be in some old folks' home writing my last will and testament. King Lear had it right, you know. 'How sharper than a serpent's tooth it is / To have a thankless child!' You know *King Lear*, do you?"

"No, ma'am." Why did she think he would know a king?

"A shame," she said, setting her teacup with a little click onto its saucer. "What Shakespeare do you know?"

"Um, none I guess. Well, I saw *Romeo and Juliet* once."

"Saw *Romeo and Juliet*? In the movies, you mean."

"Yes, ma'am. Does that count?" It made no sense that he wanted to please her, but he did.

"You must read *Lear*," she said. "But first, my mail."

It took Toby a couple of seconds to realize what she meant. "You want me to read your mail?"

"Of course. How many letters are there?"

"Two," he said, picking them up. "One from Mississippi, and one from New York."

"Toss that one," she said.

He made a wild guess. "The one from Mississippi?"

"Tear it up first."

He did what she said, tearing the envelope in half, then in half and half again.

"Music to my ears," she said. "Now read me the other one."

He felt funny reading somebody's personal mail, even

27

with permission. But the letter wasn't anything very personal. It was about a book of poems the old woman had written in 1978. As near as he could tell, the person wanted her permission to reprint the book. He said a whole lot of nice things about Pearl's poetry and hoped she was busily working on something new. The letter was signed by somebody named Abe. Yours as always, Abe. The whole thing was in actual handwriting that was almost like art.

"Never satisfied," Pearl grumbled. "Just like my children. You can toss that one, too."

"Do you write poetry? Are you a poet?" His mother read poetry books like other people read detective mysteries. Toby had never met anybody who wrote actual poems.

"I was once," she said. "All that's over now." She tightened her lips as if to keep whatever else she was going to say from getting out.

So Toby asked her what he had been going to ask in the first place, before the explosion and before he'd found her yelling at the crows. "Do you own a cow?"

"Blossom," she said. "Yes, I own that cow. As much as anybody can own a cow. Cows have minds of their own. Just like the rest of us."

"She's hungry," Toby said. "I think she's starving to death. I gave her some Cheerios—"

"Blossom? Hungry?" Pearl gave a little hoot. "She eats all day long. That's what she's standing in, son. Food."

"But she's skinny. Her ribs are sticking out."

"Well, she's no beauty queen. I'll give you that."

Geraldine jumped up on the table, sniffed at Toby's tea, and lay down in a heap on his right arm.

"But while we're on the subject of Blossom, you could give me a hand with her as well." Pearl used her stick to pull herself out of her chair. Toby thought she might be a hundred years old, but he didn't dare ask. "Ever milk a cow?"

"Me? No, ma'am. I'm from New York."

"New York has cows," said Pearl. "Millions of them."

"Not in the city they don't."

"Ah, well, more's the pity," said Pearl.

When Pearl opened the back door, there was Blossom, as if she'd been eavesdropping. Pearl laid her hand on Blossom's neck. "We've got a hired hand, old girl. What do you think about that?"

Hired hand? Did she mean him?

Blossom stuck her big nose on the side of Pearl's face, nuzzling her ear. "What is it, girl? Oh. Toby. His name is Toby. Yes, he's very nice. Go on along now. We've got to do some weeding."

4

W here have you been?"

Toby's mother was making PBJs, laying the bread slices in a row and spreading them with peanut butter thick as plaster.

"Out riding," he said.

"But that was hours ago. Where did you go?"

"Just down the road. I left you a note."

"Yes, I know you did. But it didn't say where you were going." She cut the sandwiches on the diagonal and laid them around the rim of a plate, as if they were meant for some fancy party.

"I met this old woman. Pearl. She's almost blind. She can't even read her mail, so I read it to her."

"You just ran into this woman and she asked you to read her mail?"

"Yup."

"Who is she?"

"Pearl. I just told you."

Would she never stop?

She carried the plate of sandwiches to the table and set it down. "Does she live alone?"

"Nope. Her real name is Ma Barker and she has this cool gang—"

"Oh, Toby," she said. She turned and laid her hands on his shoulders. He froze, shielding the lump with his arm. "It doesn't hurt to be careful. Sure she's old, but how do you know she isn't—" She shrugged. "I don't know."

"Crazy? A homicidal maniac?" Toby slipped his hands around his mother's neck and squeezed.

"Stop already," she said. "Get your father. Tell him lunch is ready."

Toby went over to the door and yelled for his father through the screen.

"I could have done that myself," his mother muttered.

His father came in, and they sat down to lunch as if it were something they did all the time.

"My favorite," said his father, which was what he always said. "I want to see you put on some weight this summer, Toby," he said. "You'll be playing basketball this year."

In the fall, Toby would be a sixth-grader at the same middle school his father had gone to. His father had taken him there one afternoon after all the kids were gone. They'd walked down a long, empty hallway so that Toby could see a case that was filled with trophies and old photographs. His father had pointed to a skinny guy in a crew cut and said it was him. Captain of the JV basketball team, and they hadn't lost a game, not one.

Toby took a bite of his sandwich and washed it down with milk. He never had much of an appetite. The pills had something to do with it. He thought his father knew all that. And, besides, he didn't like basketball all that much.

His mother was looking at his father incredulously.

"What?" his father said.

"Basketball?" she said.

"What?" his father said again. His mother didn't say anything. She just looked at him as if she didn't know who he was.

When they had finished eating, Toby's father went to get his duffel and they walked him out to his car. His mother and father touched their lips together. His father got in and put on his seat belt. "See you next week," he said.

"Next week we can see Mars," Toby said. "It's going to come so close to Earth you can see it with your naked eye. But we'll be able to see it better through my telescope."

"Sounds good," his father said.

After his father left, Toby went inside to check his e-mail.

Hi Toby. It sounds like you're having a great time. Cows are not my personal fave friends, but hey! You never told me who got shot or what the explosion was! Things are sort of okay here. Something popped up on an MRI so it's back to the Planet of the Dwarves for TREATment. If you don't hear from me for a while don't worry. You know how it goes. Hey, can you send me the latest Harry DVD? I'll be your best friend. Popeye

Toby stared at the screen. Planet of the Dwarves. What Popeye called Children's Hospital because everybody who checked in was short. She always made him laugh, even when it hurt to laugh. And now she was sick. Sick again. He took the Harry Potter DVD out of his duffel and set it on the desk next to his laptop. He'd ask his mom if they could put it right into the mail, but he knew that wouldn't make him feel any better.

He flopped down on his bed and stared at the ceiling. It was full of knots, knotty pine his mother said it was. The whole place was knotty.

Popeye was supposed to be cured. After her first time, she'd never had to go back for more treatment. Not like him, bouncing in and out of Children's like a yo-yo. Maybe he should have told her about his lump. When you were sick, it helped to know you weren't the only one.

Maybe he should have told her, but he couldn't. It was his. His secret, his decision.

He got up and started three e-mails to Popeye, deleting every start. They all sounded so stupid. He felt like crying or cussing or hitting something. Could he tell her that? Why couldn't he just say how sorry he was? Why was that so hard?

He turned off his laptop, got up, and slammed the desk chair into the desk, left the room intending to slam the door as well, but it wouldn't slam. Which only made him madder. But the screen door slammed all right.

"I jump out of my skin every time you do that," his mother said. She was kneeling in what she called her tomato garden.

"Sorry," said Toby, but he wasn't.

"Would you look at these poor little things? They're being eaten alive!"

The tomato plants were so puny he almost felt sorry for them. His mother leaned over, peering at their tiny leaves.

Toby sat on the steps watching her, thinking about Popeye, about himself, about the old woman, Pearl. "I've got a job," he said.

His mother sat back on her heels, wiping the sweat from her forehead with her wrist. "You what?"

"Pearl. The lady I told you about. She wants me to help her with stuff."

"What kind of *stuff*?"

Toby shrugged. "You know. Farm stuff."

"No, I don't know. Do you?"

He shrugged. "I guess not. But she's going to teach me how to milk a cow."

"You *want* to milk a cow?"

"Sure."

His mother got up and brushed the dirt off her knees.

36

"Well, I don't want you wearing yourself out," she said. "This time at the cabin is supposed to be a rest for you."

"I'm bored," he said.

"You're never bored."

She was right. How could you be bored when the world was full of a zillion things to do, and the sky had at least that many stars? "But I could get bored."

"Well, I need to meet this Pearl," his mother said.

"Why?"

Why had he told his mother about Pearl in the first place? Now she was going to butt into that.

"Because you are an eleven-year-old boy and she is a perfect stranger."

"She's an old lady. And she sure isn't perfect. Anyway, she couldn't hurt a fly."

His mother came over and sat down beside him. "You look tired," she said.

"You should see Pearl's garden," he said. "It's a *real* garden. She's got tomatoes as big as baseballs."

"Are you sleeping all right?"

Toby jumped to his feet. "Stop already!" he yelled. "Leave me alone. I'm fine. I am one hundred percent perfect! Stop asking me every minute!" He stomped across the porch and slammed back into the cabin, into his room, where he threw himself onto the bed, face-first. He wouldn't cry. He would not.

6

Here you go, Toby," said Pearl, setting the milking stool next to Blossom. "You've got to get real close."

It was Sunday morning, as good a time as any for learning to milk a cow. According to Pearl anyway.

Toby sat. He took a deep breath, closed his eyes, and laid his head against Blossom's side. Then, before he could chicken out, he reached underneath for two of her teats. They were soft and sort of rubbery, not as bad as he'd imagined.

"You got hold of them?" He could feel Pearl's breath

on the back of his neck. She was leaning over him, trying to see what he was doing.

"Got 'em," Toby said.

"Don't pull down," Pearl warned. "That's the mistake most people make. She'll bite you if you do that."

Toby froze. "She will?" How were you supposed to get the milk out without pulling on the teats?

Pearl had a deep chuckle, almost like a man's. "No, no. Blossom doesn't bite. She could give you a good kick, though."

"But what do I do if I don't pull?" There was a crick in his neck already, and he hadn't even started.

"Do just like I said. Use the last three fingers on both your hands, one teat then the other. Firm but gentle pressure, that's the trick. Gentle the milk out of her. Isn't that right, girl?"

Blossom slowly turned her head toward Pearl. A sound came from her throat that made Toby jump and lose the one teat he'd gotten a firm but gentle grip on.

"He'll catch on, girl. Be still now."

Toby started as Geraldine wove between his ankles, turned, and made another pass. A fly landed on his ear.

"There's no milk coming out," Toby said. "I don't think I'm doing it right."

"There's no hurry, child. You can't make it happen. You have to let it happen."

Let it happen? What was she talking about? Why didn't she just tell him what he was doing wrong?

Blossom shuffled her back feet, Toby pressed tighter with the fingers of his right hand, and out shot the milk, hitting the bucket with a solid ping.

"That's it," said Pearl. "Just keep doing what you're doing. Make sure to milk her till she's clean. Then come on up to the house." He heard her thump away, leaving him alone with Blossom.

It was much harder than he thought, milking a cow. Instead of pouring in a nice steady stream, the milk shot and squirted everywhere, over the sides of the bucket and soaking his sneakers. It didn't help that you couldn't see what you were doing, and that the cow didn't seem to want you there. Or that your right hand got a cramp in it, which made you let go of the teat. And that, grabbing for another, you knocked the bucket over, spilling what little milk you had collected all over the floor.

It wasn't one bit of fun milking a cow. It was plain hard work.

Blossom made that sound in her throat again. "Settle down, girl," Toby said gruffly, as if he'd been bossing cows around all his life. Blossom lowed again; this time the lowing sounded more like a laugh. Then something just settled inside of Toby, and his hands began to draw the milk from the cow, sure and steady. For a little while, time and Toby and Blossom were one working thing. Flies buzzed, crows cawed, but the cow stood still. She'd even stopped laughing at him.

Pearl came to the back door, and Toby handed her the bucket. She shook it, gauging how much milk there was by the sound of the slosh.

"I didn't get it all," Toby said. "Some spilled—"

"No use crying over—" Her mouth turned up a little at the corners. "Well, you know the rest. Come inside. There's this poem I've been wanting to read."

Then Toby was on a ladder laid against one of the dusty bookshelves. One by one, he read the titles on the spines of the old books: *Collected Poems of Thomas Hardy*, *The Annotated Shakespeare* Vol. I, *Pride and Prejudice*. He read all down one row, then started the next.

"Keep going," she'd say whenever he would pause or sneeze, which he did again and again because of the dust. Finally, when he got to a skinny little book called *The Shadow Heart*, she said, "That's it. Bring that one down."

She sure didn't mind telling a person what to do.

Toby climbed down the ladder with the book stuck under his arm.

He was covered with dust. There was dust every-where you looked. She probably didn't even know it was there, covering everything with a coat of gray fur. Should he tell her? What a job that would be, dusting all the old furniture. He decided not to. Dust wasn't exactly dangerous, he figured, unless it filled up the room.

" 'Should There Be a Day,' " Pearl said. "Find that one."

Toby ran his finger down the list of poems in the contents. " 'Should There Be a Day,' " he read. "It's on page twenty-one."

"Ah, yes, lovely poem. Bring it into the kitchen, where you can see to read it," she said.

In the kitchen, he pressed the book open on the table. Then he cleared his throat, and, as if he were about to make a speech, or march off to war, began to read. " 'Should there be a day. When you are not. And I am yet with breath. What shall I say. What shall I ask of death? Come get the rest. The half of me that stays. Shallow of heart, hollow as a bone? Or shall I determine to forget. Delight entombed—' "

"Oh, dear," Pearl said.

Toby looked up from the words he was reading so carefully. He knew what most of them meant all right, but how they went together was sort of weird. *Delight entombed?* "What's wrong?"

"Well, poetry is all about stopping at the right places," she said. "Just because you come to the end of a line doesn't mean you have to stop there. Stop at the periods, just like you do anywhere else. Now begin again. And don't rush through it. Savor the words."

Toby did what she said, trying his best to savor the words, whatever that meant. He could hardly understand what the poet was trying to say, or why, if she was trying to say something important, she didn't just say it straight. The *sun of truth*? *What of me is you?*

It was worse than milking a cow, reading poetry. It was like trying to understand Chinese.

From another room came the ringing of a telephone. "Read it again, will you?" Pearl said. "More slowly this time. And the word is en-toom-ed not en-tome-ed."

"The phone's ringing," Toby said.

"Yes, of course it is," she said. "You can wait until it stops if you'd like."

The telephone rang and rang. Toby began counting the rings. Eighteen, nineteen, twenty . . .

"They'll give up eventually," she said.

"Who?"

"My children."

"Oh." The phone stopped ringing at thirty-three.

"They won't leave me alone," she said. "Ninety-four years on this earth and they want to run my life. Get off the table, Geraldine."

The cat made a rusty meow.

"What? Well, I don't care if your feet are cold. Go sit in the sun."

The cat threw Pearl a disgusted look and hopped down off the table. Toby coughed away a laugh. Was Pearl crazy? Did she really think the cat could understand people talk? And Blossom. She treated Blossom like a person she'd been having regular conversations with. He should have known the old woman was crazy that first day, when he saw the strange sign on her door.

"It was my oven that got them going," Pearl said. "None of their business if it blew up."

"You blew up your oven?"

"Should have smelled the gas," she muttered as if to herself, shaking her head. "Got to thinking about something else. Could have happened to anybody."

Toby didn't think so. Sure, it was an old-fashioned stove, the kind you had to light with a match. But he didn't think people with old stoves like hers went around blowing them up. She was lucky she hadn't blown herself up and the whole house, too.

"We should settle our accounts," Pearl said. "Would you like to be paid each day, or would the end of the week be all right?"

She'd caught Toby by surprise. "You don't have to pay me," he said.

"Two dollars an hour is what I told Mitchell."

"Mitchell?"

"The grocer. The one who sent you over."

"Nobody sent me over," Toby said. "I just came by to tell you about Blossom."

Pearl's mouth dropped open. "Mitchell didn't send you?"

"No, ma'am."

"Then why—? Oh, my dear child. Why on earth—?"

"It's okay," he said quickly. "I like Blossom. And poetry's not so bad."

Pearl began to laugh, and for a moment that was almost like magic, Toby saw a younger Pearl, all her lines turning up instead of down. She laughed until tears ran in little rivers over her wrinkled face. Then she pulled a tissue out of her sleeve and blew her nose, a good hard honk. "Now if that isn't something!" she said. "So then, Toby, tell me all about yourself. If you've come to be my friend and not my hired hand, we must know more about each other."

So Toby told her about the cabin where his family was staying, said that his mother was a cellist with the symphony, that his father was a real estate broker, and that he himself was going into middle school and wanted someday to become an astronomer.

Everything but what she didn't need to know.

45

"Is your mother aware that you're here?" she asked, more gently now that they were friends.

He told her that she was, but that she expected him home for lunch.

"You'd better be on your way then." She got up, so he did, too. She thumped along behind him to the door. Opening it, he saw the sign again.

"What does this mean?" Since they were friends, he figured he had the right to ask.

"My sign? Means what it says. You know what freedom is."

"Yes, ma'am."

"Well, you lose it when you get old," she said, "if you're not careful. Folks want to move right in and take over, tell you this and that thing. Where to go and what to do. You get old, you lose your rights, that's what."

"Oh," said Toby. He didn't know what else to say. How could he understand how it was to be old? He was only a kid. But the sound of a screen door slamming came back to him, along with the sound of his own angry voice. *Stop already! Leave me alone!* His mother's mouth had opened as if she'd been going to speak, but then she'd shut it again. She'd blinked a lot like she'd been going to cry. His father always backed down when his mother cried. But Toby wasn't about to back down. She could cry all she wanted, he wasn't going to let her run his life anymore. He knew what freedom was all right.

"Don't mind the sign," Pearl said. "It's as much for me as anything else. It's not meant to scare decent folks away."

"No, ma'am."

"Milking's gotten real hard for me," she said. "I could use your help. Blossom could, too. She says it's hard to think with all that milk weighing her down."

"She doesn't really talk, right?"

Pearl smiled. "Blossom? Sure she does. She's a cow full of the most wonderful secrets."

"Secrets?" Toby's mouth begin to twitch. He fought the urge to laugh. "Secrets about what?"

"Oh, the meaning of life. That sort of thing."

"She's some cow," Toby said.

"She sure is," Pearl agreed.

Toby walked away fast, before Pearl could hear him cracking up.

1

Milking Blossom wasn't any easier the next day. First he tried squeezing one way, then another. Not a single squirt. Blossom's hair prickled his cheek and smelled like the rest of the barn, like hay and he didn't know what all. Cow poop, though he didn't want to think too much about that. She was warm and it was a cool morning. He'd never worked so hard, or tried so hard not to make it be work. To let it happen, like Pearl said. And then he just stopped thinking about it. His hands began to squeeze as if they'd always known how. And, sure enough, the milk began to flow.

Pearl had caught cold. Earlier, when Toby had knocked on her door, she'd answered wrapped to her ears in a tattered quilt. "Can you light that old stove?" she asked, raspy-voiced. "I could use a cup of lemon tea."

Toby said sure, he could light the stove. He could make her a cup of tea, too. He'd made tea for his mother sometimes, but he didn't tell Pearl that. It was only when he wanted his mother to agree to something.

"Milk Blossom first," Pearl said. "She's been complaining all morning. Don't know what's wrong with her."

Sick old ladies, sick cows. His mother would have a stroke.

Toby listened to the steady ping-ping of the milk against the sides of the bucket. His aim was getting better. A bee, humming like a tiny machine, flew several loops around his head and flew off again. Blossom chewed her cud like it was a big wad of bubblegum. Toby began thinking about the night before, when he'd told his mother that Popeye (his mother called her Susan) was sick again. His mother had promised to send the DVD this morning from the little post office that was stuck in the back of the market. Overnight mail, she'd said, if they had such a thing.

Then she'd gotten very quiet.

Later when he'd seen the way she was staring out the

window at the lake, he was sorry he'd told her. Should have ridden his bike to the post office and mailed the DVD himself. Why hadn't he thought of that first?

He took the milk up to the house, laid the bucket on the steps, and sat down to take off his sneakers. He didn't want to add to the mess on Pearl's kitchen floor. Maybe her children were worried about her living in such a messy house. Maybe that was why she was so mad at them, because they wouldn't let her live in dirt, if that was what she wanted.

The burner lit with a little pop. Toby found a Lemon Mist teabag in a canister by the stove and put it into one of the flowered teacups. The hardest part was carrying the cup into the living room without spilling the hot tea into the saucer.

Pearl was tucked into a corner of the dusty green couch. She reached for the saucer, then started to cough. Waving him away with one hand, she coughed and hacked into the other. Toby stood like a butler holding her tea.

"Thank you, Toby," she said when her coughing fit was over. "Sit down, sit down. Don't worry, I'm not going to die on you."

She'd read his mind. It made him feel bad. But she was just so *old*.

"We're going to read some Frost today," she said. "How would you like that?"

He didn't know how to answer. He guessed she meant a poem. About winter probably. Would he like it? The odds were not good.

"In the blue book," she said, pointing a shaky finger. "It's called 'The Road Not Taken.' You probably know it."

Toby found the poem. It was in a long list of poems by a poet called Robert Frost. He felt a little silly then for thinking it would be a poem about winter. It was the poet's name, and he was probably a very famous poet, too.

"Are some of your poems in here?" he asked Pearl as she waited, hands folded, for him to begin reading.

"Oh, heavens no," she said. "Forget about me. I don't write poetry anymore." Her face soured and she looked away. So Toby began to read to her, remembering to stop only if he came to a period, which wasn't until the third part, more than halfway through the whole poem. By then, he was out of breath.

"Easy now," Pearl said. "You read like a horse heading for the barn. Listen to the words, what he's saying. Go back to the beginning. Then tell me what you see."

"What I see?" Words, that was what he saw. Black print on white paper. What was he *supposed* to see?

"After," she said. "Tell me what your mind saw."

Toby paid more attention to the words this time. Some were strange, like "yellow wood." And then suddenly he saw the whole thing. It was like the time they'd gone up to see his grandpa in Vermont. It was in the late fall and the leaves had all turned. It wasn't exactly a yellow wood, it was more like Pearl's quilt, a patchwork of fading color. But Toby could see it just the same. He could see the traveler standing there, trying to make up his mind about which way to go.

"Well?" Pearl said when he'd come to the end of the poem.

Toby told her what he'd seen. "But why is it such a big deal which way he goes?"

"Well, it's hard to make decisions sometimes. I expect he knows he could go either way, but he has to choose. And he wants to choose right."

"How does he know which one's right?"

"I think his heart tells him," said Pearl. "Don't you find that's true?"

8

Pearl's sick," he told his mother, who was scrubbing a cutting board hard enough to wear a hole through it. Steam rose from a big pot on the burner. All the way home, Toby had thought about Pearl alone in her broken-down house. He didn't even care if his mother got mad that he'd read to her and made her a cup of tea, knowing he could catch her cold. That he'd "compromised his health" was how she would put it.

"How did I know somebody was sick?" his mother said.

"Huh?"

She nodded in the direction of the pot. "Chicken soup. We'll take some over to her."

Toby groaned.

"What's wrong?"

"Nothing."

"We'll mail the DVD to Susan on the way," she said.

"You didn't mail it yet?"

"Toby. It's nine o'clock. The post office doesn't open until nine."

Nothing about catching Pearl's cold. Maybe she'd cut him some slack for once.

"I want you to wear your mask," she said.

"To the post office?" For three months after his last treatment, he'd worn the paper mask over his nose and mouth every time he left the house. He'd hated breathing his own used-up breath, almost more than he hated the looks he got.

"Just when you're at Pearl's," she said. "We don't want you compromising—"

"I know, I know."

"Nice car," his mother said, pulling up behind a sleek silver car in Pearl's driveway. "You didn't tell me Pearl had such a fancy car. New, too."

"It's not hers," he said. "I *told* you she's almost blind. How could she drive?"

Toby's mother turned off the ignition. "Toby?"

"What?"

"Are you still mad at me?"

"No." And then because he knew he really was: "Yeah."

"Because I worry about you?"

"Because you're always . . . *bugging* me!" he said. "See that sign on the door?" He pointed at Pearl's door with the faded blue paint and her hand-lettered sign lifting and settling in the breeze.

His mother squinched her eyes trying to read it.

Toby read it to her. "Whoever steals my freedom takes my life."

Toby's mother was quiet for a little bit. "So I'm stealing your freedom, is that it? I am stealing freedom from my eleven-year-old son?" She dragged out the eleven-year-old part, like there was a period between every word.

"The soup's getting cold," Toby said. "Can't we just go in?"

His mother made a noise through her nose and opened her door. Then she came around and opened the door for him. Toby got out, carrying the hot soup.

A tall, thin lady in a red suit opened Pearl's door. Her black hair was pulled back so tight that it made her eyes skinny. "Yes?"

Toby's mother turned her charm on like a light switch, explaining what she and Toby were doing there holding a pot of soup. The lady looked down her long, thin nose, first at Toby, at his mask, then his bald head. Then she spoke directly to his mother. "Come in," she said at last. "Mother is feeling much better."

They followed Pearl's daughter through the living room. Toby's mother looked everywhere, her caterpillars on full alert. He knew without her saying it exactly what she thought. Pearl's daughter disappeared into the kitchen.

In the room with Pearl was another dark-haired, long-nosed lady. This one wore jeans and a red sweatshirt.

"This is my twin sister, Miranda," said the one in the suit. "I am Cassandra. We're Pearl's family. All she has."

"According to you," said Pearl, scowling. "*All* I have. Hmmmph!"

Toby introduced his mother to Pearl, who was glowering at her daughters like a captured witch. His mother said all the right things about all the good things Toby had said about Pearl, which was only half true. He hadn't told her much of anything.

"We'll just leave you with the soup," his mother said. "Toby didn't know your family was coming."

"Neither did I," Pearl muttered. Then she said something about bad pennies turning up that Toby didn't quite catch.

"Cassandra got a feeling about Mother—" "Miranda got a feeling about Mother—" they said at once.

"I get feelings, too," said Pearl. "Ever consider my feelings? You could have called."

"We did call, Mother," Miranda said.

"But you didn't answer," said Cassandra.

"Must have called the wrong number," Pearl said, turning back to Toby and his mother. "They brought a lemon meringue pie. Would you like some pie?"

"No, thank you," his mother said. "We'll just be go—"

"It's store-bought," Pearl said. "Probably tastes like the box it came out of."

"*Mo*ther," Cassandra said.

"*Mo*ther," Miranda said.

"*Mo*ther," said Pearl, in a raspy voice.

"You see how she is—" Miranda said.

"Won't listen to a word we say," said Cassandra.

Then both ladies started talking at once, complaining about Pearl. "She refuses to leave this dump . . . perfectly wonderful room in my home . . . in *my* home . . . acts as if we're hauling her off to jail . . . one of those grim retirement . . . doesn't see a thing, you know . . . doesn't hear all that well either . . ."

"I do, too! I hear just fine. Not a thing wrong with

57

my hearing! Behave yourselves. Toby's mother doesn't want to listen to your whining. And neither does Toby."

She winked at Toby.

The daughters yammered on.

When Toby heard the words "court order," he whirled around.

"Oh, I don't think—" his mother was saying.

"Oh, yes, perfectly legal," said Miranda.

"Perfectly," said Cassandra.

"What's a court order?" said Toby.

Both daughters looked at Toby as if he'd grown a second bald head.

"They think they're going to remove me from the premises," Pearl said. "Declare my house a firetrap and haul me away."

"My dad's an attorney," Toby said, yanking off his mask. "He won't let—"

"Toby," his mother warned, whether about keeping his mask on or lying about his father's occupation, he didn't know which. And didn't care.

"You can't make her move," he said. "Pearl doesn't want to move!"

"Atta boy," Pearl cried. "You tell 'em!"

"Toby, this isn't any of our business," his mother said. "I'm sorry, but Toby is very fond of Pearl. He's been over here every day and, well, they've become friends."

The daughters frowned. "This has nothing to do with friendship," said Miranda.

"It has to do with *family*," said Cassandra.

His mother looked as if she was going to say something. But then she laid a hand on Toby's shoulder. "Let's go, honey."

"I'll be back tomorrow, Pearl," Toby said. "I'll be back to milk Blossom." Hard as it was to point his finger at both daughters at once, and even though he knew it was rude, he did it just the same. "And Pearl had better be here."

9

Toby kicked up a rooster tail of dust skidding into Pearl's driveway. The house looked exactly the same as it had the day before, the shades drawn, her note still on the door. If Pearl was gone, wouldn't the house look somehow *different*?

Laying his bike down, he ran up to the door. He knocked three times, no answer. Remembering what Pearl's daughters had said about her hearing, he began to hammer with the side of his hand. "Pearl? Pearl?" He leaped off the stone step and ran around the side of the house. "Pearl?"

"Back here. In the barn!"

Filled with relief, Toby hurried toward the barn. Pearl was here! She'd escaped the clutches of the evil twins.

At first he thought the cow had fallen over. He'd only seen Blossom on her feet and figured she slept that way, like horses did most of the time. But here she was stretched out on her side, Pearl on the milking stool next to her.

"Is she sick?" Toby whispered, as if he were in a hospital room. He took off his helmet and knelt beside Blossom.

"I'm not sure," said Pearl. "Something's not right, but if she knows she isn't telling. Are you, girl? Is this one secret you're keeping to yourself?"

Blossom closed her eyes and scratched her face against the hay-strewn dirt.

"I've called the vet," Pearl said. "He'll come and check her over. But she'd be more comfortable in the meantime if she was milked." So Pearl and Toby did what they could to convince Blossom she needed to get up. Pearl promised her sugar, Toby tried lifting her big head. But when she rolled a dark eye up at him and lowed, Toby could see she just wanted to be left alone.

"That's all right, girl," Pearl said. "Yes, yes, we'll let you rest awhile. What's that you say? Oh, you're not so old," she scoffed. "I'm a lot older than you and I'm still kicking." She smoothed one of Blossom's big ears between her fingers. Then she stood. "We'll let her be," she said to Toby, who hung back, not wanting to leave Blossom.

"Come," Pearl said. Toby felt her hand land lightly as a bird on his bare head. For a little while, nothing moved, not Pearl, not Blossom, not Toby. The barn was as quiet as night, as if it, too, were waiting. Then Pearl said "come" again, more quietly this time, and Toby got up. He followed her out of the barn.

She knew.

Things would change now.

She would treat him the way everybody else did, even his parents, who were supposed to know better. She would treat him like a sick person.

She stopped outside the barn, squinting in the sunshine. He could see she was thinking hard. "I could use some eggs for my dinner," she said at last. "Let's see if any of the girls are laying."

It took a second or two for Toby's mind to change gears. Then he took off after her in the direction of the chicken yard.

The minute Pearl released the latch on the gate, the chickens went crazy. Some ran in circles, others tried to fly, all of them cackled like they were about to be murdered in the snow of their own feathers. "Look inside and see who's roosting," Pearl said.

Toby bent down, looked into the shelter where the nests were. A white hen lifted her head, then turned it to look at him as if she had only one good eye. The eye was yellow and peered at him suspiciously.

"Who's in there?" Pearl said.

"I don't know," Toby said. "One of them's white. A white chicken."

"All white? Or does she have some gray feathers on the side?"

It was dark inside the shelter. "Just white, I think."

"Belinda," Pearl said. "She'll let us have an egg. I'll tell her about Blossom. Put your hand under her and slip an egg out. Slowly."

Toby stuck his hand into the shelter. Belinda cackled, ruffled her feathers. Toby sneezed. Belinda shot straight up off the nest. Toby snatched the one egg she'd been sitting on.

"Settle down, Belinda," Pearl said. "Yes, I know, I know. He's new at all this. No, he didn't mean it. Did you, Toby?"

"Didn't mean what?"

"Didn't mean to be so rough. She said you swiped that egg just like that double-dealing, egg-snatching fox."

Toby looked down at the egg cradled in his hand. "I'm sorry, Belinda," he said. *What was he doing apologizing to a chicken?*

Pearl had a different trick for each of the hens. One

could be distracted by food, another by poetry. By the time they were finished, there were six eggs. Enough for the week, Pearl said.

If Pearl could make an omelet, didn't that mean she could take care of herself? Toby didn't much like that he was beginning to see her through the evil twins' eyes, and maybe his mother's as well. Pearl had a right to live her life any way she wanted to, for as long as she was able. But what would happen when he was gone?

If his parents knew about the lump, he would already be gone, back at Children's. All the more reason to keep it a secret.

The poem for the day was about two horses in a field that the poet kept confusing with flowers. Other than that, it was a pretty nice poem. Toby made tea. This time he decided to try the Raspberry Delight, but it, too, tasted like straw. He didn't see what people got out of drinking tea. He thought it might be nothing more than a silly habit left over from England.

Pearl set her cup in its saucer. "This may be none of my business, Toby," she said.

Here it comes, Toby said to himself. Pearl was just like everybody else, after all. She had to hear what was wrong with him. Even though she knew, she had to know. A kid didn't lose his hair for no reason.

Well, he would tell her the truth. He lied to his mother, but only because he had to. He wouldn't lie to Pearl.

"Are your parents still together?"

Relief flooded Toby the way it had when he'd heard Pearl's voice call out from the barn. "Together? My folks? Sure!"

"Oh, well, none of my business, as I said. It's just that you talk about your mother, but you haven't said anything about your father—"

So Toby explained about his father working all week in the city and that he tried to come up on the weekends but couldn't always.

"I see," she said. "Well, they're very fortunate to have such a nice young man for a son. But I suppose they know that."

There was a knock on the door. "That'll be Doc Homann," Pearl said. "Answer it, will you?" She struggled to her feet, using her stick for support.

The vet looked like his father's mechanic without the grease. He wore overalls like Pearl's and had big beefy-looking arms. His handshake squeezed the life out of Toby's hand. Just for a second he had glanced at Toby's head the same way everybody else did, but it was hard to tell what he was thinking. "This your grandson, Pearl?"

"Wish I could claim him," Pearl said. "But no, he's

just on loan I'm afraid. He's my right-hand man these days. Don't know what I'd do without him."

Doc Homann smiled at Toby, lifting his bushy eyebrows. "Well, let's take a look at that cow," he said.

When they got to the barn, Blossom was on her feet, like somebody had warned her that the doctor was coming and she'd better shape up. She stuck her big nose in the vet's ear, but if she told him anything the vet wasn't letting on. He listened to her heart, went around the back of her with a giant thermometer and checked her temperature. Last, he opened her mouth and stuck his hand inside.

Toby thought Blossom was very good about all of this, a better patient than he had ever been.

"Well, she's a gummer, you know," Doc Homann said, putting away his instruments. "Not much we can do about that. No fever. Heart normal enough for a cow her age."

"What's a gummer?" Toby asked Pearl when the vet was gone.

"She's worn her teeth down to the gums," Pearl said. "So she can't chew her cud anymore. Best she can do is mash it around some."

"It's good she isn't sick, huh?"

Pearl looked out across the field, as if she'd gotten a

glimpse of somebody coming, a stranger maybe. Then she looked at Toby and her eyes cleared. "Yes, it's good she isn't feeling poorly," she said.

But Blossom wasn't her old self, not the next day, or the next, or the day after that. Her spot at the fence was empty, as if a cow had never been there at all.

10

Each day, even though he wanted to stay longer at Pearl's, Toby would always ride back to the cabin in time for lunch. If he didn't, his mother would start to fret. He could tell she was trying hard not to bug him, but she just couldn't help herself. She was a mother and mothers worried. Toby was tired a lot, and that was hard to hide, especially if he fell asleep in the chair on the porch. He'd wake up with drool running down his chin and his mother watching over him like a fearful hen.

In the evenings, they'd play chess or read their books. But sometimes Toby's mind would wander off and he would start to worry, too. Not so much about himself but about Blossom and Pearl and Popeye. He'd already made up his mind about himself, but there was little he could do for any of them. Only then could he see his mother as the nice person she was, and not the nag he made her out to be.

On Friday afternoon, Toby had just begun a jigsaw puzzle of the Great Wall of China when he heard his father's car. His mother was at the sink washing a mess of dirty spinach from the farmers' market. "Dad's here," he said.

Toby went with his mother out onto the porch.

"What traffic!" his father said, tromping up the steps. He and Toby's mother touched lips. "Took me five and a half hours. Hey, guy!"

His father crouched, and Toby got ready for the punch that was never a real punch.

"Do you *have* to do that?" Toby's mother said.

"What?" said his father.

"That stupid boxing thing. If you're glad to see each other, can't you just hug?"

"Like this?" Toby's father caught him in a bear hug so fast Toby couldn't put his arms where they needed to be. He struggled to get free. "Let go, Dad!" His father's arms relaxed. His hands slid down, over Toby's ribs. Then the left one stopped. Toby watched his father's face freeze, felt the big hand stay right where it was, over the lump. Toby backed away.

"Toby?"

Toby turned and went into the cabin, catching the door behind him so that it made no noise at all when it closed. Then he went into his room and closed that door, too. He wished there were fifty other doors to close between him and his parents, between him and them and what was going to happen next.

11

Toby checked his e-mail. Nothing but spam. Nothing from Popeye. He paced his little room like a prisoner, even though the door wasn't locked. He could open it and walk right out. And there would be his jailers, his mother and father, waiting to deal with his crime and the cover-up. He'd lied to them, that was what they'd say. He had told them over and over again he was fine, when clearly he was not.

It wasn't their anger that kept him in his room. Like a storm, it would sound scary for a while, but it would soon blow over and things would get back to normal.

Only normal could never be normal for him. His mother would call his oncologist, his father would call the people who rented them the cabin, both of them would start packing up. They would stop seeing him, standing in the middle of it all like . . . like another *thing* to take care of.

They loved him, he never doubted that. But if they didn't love him so hard and so tightly, maybe they could see him better.

Toby turned out his desk light and climbed under the blankets with all his clothes on. He stuck a pillow over his head.

When he awoke he thought it was morning, and that his mother, for once, was up before he was.

"Toby? Honey?" Followed by her soft knock on his door.

He sat up. Outside his window, a wash of stars across a black sky. "What?"

"May I come in?"

"Okay." In his dream he'd been chasing a rabbit through a cornfield, and he was still out of breath.

His mom came in and sat down at the end of his bed, a dark figure surrounded by stars.

He asked her what time it was.

"Two," she said. "After two. Dad's going to drive back to the city tonight, get things started. He'll be in to say goodbye in a minute."

"Okay."

"We're not mad, Toby," she said. "Daddy and I aren't angry with you."

"That's good."

"We're just . . . I don't know. Sad, I guess. Disappointed."

"It's okay if you're mad," he said.

Anger was better than disappointment any old time. You could be angry back at somebody who was angry with you, but what could you do about disappointment? Be disappointed back?

"Why didn't you tell us, honey? All these days . . . !"

"I was going to," he said, another lie. Lies were piling up like the wood stacked against the fireplace.

His father came in, a dark silhouette in the open door. "Car's loaded. You'll just have to take what's left, your clothes, whatever."

Toby's mother blew her nose. Only then did Toby know she'd been weeping. She got up and left the room.

His father sat down on the bed. "Now I don't want you worrying, son. Things are taken care of. We'll get you back into treatment and, hey! it will all be over in a couple of months, right?"

"Sure," Toby said. He looked from his father out at the night sky. "We never got to look at Mars," he said.

"Oh," his father said, as if this was the first he'd heard of it. "Right. Well, come on. Let's have a look-see."

"Now?"

"Isn't this the best time? It's dark, right?"

"Well, yeah, I guess," Toby said. He got up. His father pulled the bed over to the window so that they could sit on the edge. He set the telescope between them.

Toby swung the instrument down and stuck his eye against the eyepiece. When he adjusted the focus, the stars came to meet him, shimmering like ice crystals in a black sea, swarms and clusters of stars, too many ever to count.

The night before, he had done just this, and the night before that. He'd known where Mars was, knew where to find it. But somehow he didn't go there, didn't want to see the planet then. When he saw Mars for the first time, he wanted his father beside him.

And there it was, Mars in all his glory. Mars the great warrior, spinning alone in space. Toby's breath caught in his chest.

"Look, Dad!" Toby said. He turned from the telescope and saw, before his father could brush them away, the tears that were streaming down his face.

"It's okay, Dad," Toby said. It was all he could think to say. It was what his father always said to him.

His father cleared his throat. He sniffed and cleared his throat again. Then he reached over and gripped Toby's knee. "Let's see that thing," he said, and reached for the telescope.

12

Saturday morning, when Toby's mother came out to the porch with her cup of coffee, Toby was sitting on the steps.

"Oh!" she said. "I'm glad you're here. I thought you'd probably gone to Pearl's to say goodbye."

"Nope."

"Well, I've got some good news and some bad news. There won't be a bed for you until Tuesday. Daddy says that's okay. He doesn't like us driving down in the week-end traffic anyway. We'll have a little more time in our cabin."

"Mom?"

"Hmmm?" She gathered her robe around her knees and sat beside him on the step.

"I'm not going to do it."

She looked over at him, puzzled. "Do what?"

"Treatment."

"*Toby!*"

"I'm not."

"What are you talking about? Of course you are."

Toby fought to keep his voice steady and calm. "No, I'm not. It's my life and I'm not going back in there."

A laugh came out of his mother like she'd been punched. She stood up and crossed her arms. "Is this more of that freedom stuff? What's Pearl been feeding you anyway? What kind of nonsense is this? Of course you're going into treatment." Her words rained down, striking his head like little bombs.

He stood up. "Now I'm going to Pearl's," he said. He strode off toward his bicycle.

"Toby! Toby, you come back here this minute! Come back here, young man!"

Toby climbed onto his bike and sailed down the drive.

He'd done it! He'd told her. The wind flew over his helmetless head as Toby whipped past the fields, faster than he'd ever pedaled before. He'd told her!

He hadn't told his dad. That was all right. Smart. His

dad would have wrapped him up in a blanket, thrown him in the back of his car, and driven a hundred miles an hour straight into the Children's Hospital parking lot.

Well, he wouldn't have done that. But it was hard to predict what his father would do. His mother was easy. She would just talk. And talk. And talk. She would expect him to come round, to see things her way, to be reasonable.

Well, he was tired of being reasonable. Now he was going to be free.

He found Pearl with Blossom in the barn.

"She's not doing so well," Pearl said. "She says it's her time."

"Her time?"

"To move on, she says."

Toby's knees got wobbly, and he sat in a heap beside Blossom. "You mean she's going to die?"

"Well, that isn't how she put it. But, yes, it comes to the same thing. She's very delicate about d-e-a-t-h." Pearl's voice had dropped to a whisper.

Toby whispered back, "She can't spell?"

"Did you ever know a cow that could spell?"

Toby rolled his eyes. "No! But I never knew a cow who could talk either."

"Well, she is a special cow, I'll grant you that."

They both looked at Blossom, as if they expected her to join the conversation.

"How does she know she's going to d-i-e?"

Blossom lowed, her tail slapped the ground.

"Shall I tell him about India, girl?" Pearl asked. She listened for a minute. Toby did, too, but the only sound in the barn came from the flies. "Yes, she'd like that," Pearl said. "She'd like to hear all about India again."

So Pearl told Toby the story of Blossom's life in India, how she'd lived in the royal household and been treated as well as any of the raja's children. She'd been taken to festivals decked in the finest silk and pearls. A banquet of her favorite foods had been set before her on her first birthday, and then every birthday after that.

"How did she get all the way here?" Toby asked.

"Oh, that was in her other life," Pearl said. "The one before this."

"She had a whole other life? Like she died"—he lowered his voice—"d-i-e-d and came back again?"

"Oh, yes," said Pearl, "Blossom's lived many lives. She's a very old soul, aren't you, girl? An old, old soul. But her best life was the one in India."

"It's called reinvention, right?"

Pearl chuckled. "Well, yes, that's a good word for it. Reincarnation some call it." Pearl leaned on Toby's shoulder to get to her feet.

"Do you believe in that stuff?" Toby said. "In reincarnation?"

Pearl smiled. "I'd rather have all my lives right here on Earth," said Pearl. "I've been blessed with so many, as a child, a young woman, a wife and mother—"

"A poet," said Toby.

"Hmmph," said Pearl.

"I wanted to be an astronaut once," said Toby.

"And don't you still?"

"Sure," said Toby. "Only . . ."

"Only what?"

"I got sick," he said.

"And then you got better," Pearl said.

"It's not like a whole new life or anything," Toby said, even though it felt like one sometimes.

"It isn't?" said Pearl.

While Blossom rested, Toby helped Pearl gather vegetables. She wanted him to take some home with him. The garden smelled like the farmers' market, only better. There were real bugs in it, too. Toby thought about the tomato plants his mother had tried so hard to grow. He could ask Pearl about them, but what was the use now? No one would be here to pick the tomatoes. It was the end of their vacation. His lump had seen to that. He plucked one of Pearl's fat red tomatoes and set it in his basket.

"I told the girls to take some vegetables with them

when they were here, but they didn't bother. Never saw such a thing as Miranda's freezer, filled to the top with frozen peas and corn, and those cardboard television dinners!"

The evil twins.

"Are they going to take you away from here?" Toby said.

"Oh, they've threatened to do as much a hundred times. They really don't want me living with them any more than I want to live with them. But they don't want anything to happen to me either." Pearl chuckled her deep chuckle. "So they're stuck."

"They won't get a court order?"

"Oh, dear, no. I can't imagine anything like that. Smell this cilantro." Pearl stuck a bunch of green leafy stuff under his nose.

"Wow," Toby said when the strong, spicy smell took over his nose, then his whole head.

"There's lots of wow in this garden," she said.

Toby followed Pearl down the row, filling his basket.

"Pearl?"

"Yes?"

"Do you think a kid's parents could get a court order to make him do something?"

"Well, I don't know," said Pearl. She turned and squinted up at Toby. "I suppose it would depend upon what that something is."

"I have cancer," Toby said.

Pearl looked at him through her milky eyes. "Yes, I suspected that was it. It's come back, has it?"

Toby touched his side and nodded. He could feel the hot tears gathering.

"Let's go inside, Toby. We'll have our tea."

Pearl put the kettle on, then she chased Geraldine off the table and sat down beside Toby. She took his hand in both of hers. He kept swallowing so that he wouldn't cry. "What happens now?" she said.

"We're going home. Only I'm not going back to the hospital."

"No?"

Toby felt his mouth pinch hard against his anger. "Nope."

"What will happen then?"

Toby shrugged. "If I don't get treatment? I'll d-i-e," he said. "I guess."

"I see," she said softly. Her hand was still, a shell laid over his.

"Maybe I'll come back as a megamillionaire." Toby felt his face trying to laugh, but it didn't quite work. "Or a cow."

"Well, it's something to think about, isn't it?" Pearl said, as if Toby was making sense.

"I don't want to be sick anymore," said Toby. He pulled his hand back and made a fist of it. "They make you sick to make you better. It's awful!" He waited for her to tell him he was being stupid. But he wasn't, and she didn't say it. "The stem cell thing might not even work," he cried. "Like they can never say for sure! And getting ready for it is worse than anything! All the stuff you've got to take for weeks. At home. In the hospital."

Toby spit out the names of all the drugs he knew as well as he knew the alphabet, the ones he choked down, then couldn't keep down. The ones that made him shake with chills or burn with fever. The ones that pounded on his head or made his throat so sore he couldn't talk. Cyclophosphamide, doxorubicin, vincristine, cisplatin. He told Pearl about his first time at Children's, when all he saw coming and going were knees. He was that little. He felt all over again how frightened he'd been. And how sad he'd been afterward. How, instead of going back to kindergarten after Christmas with his best pals, Billy and Andy, he'd had to stay at home in bed. By the time he got back to school, he had no best friends. "I was like this . . . this *alien*!"

Pearl's old face was sad and peaceful all at the same time. He let the words pour out of him and onto her. All the anger and sadness trapped inside came spilling out. "It isn't fair!" he cried.

"No," said Pearl, "it isn't fair."

Toby wiped his hand across his wet face. "I hate being a baby," he said.

"Tears are a blessing, child," said Pearl. "A relief and a blessing. I read sad poems sometimes just to give myself the pleasure of crying."

"You do?"

"Oh, yes."

Toby sort of knew what was coming.

"Do you feel like reading a poem?" said Pearl.

"Not a sad poem."

"No," said Pearl, "though I suppose it wouldn't hurt."

It took Toby a while to find the book she wanted, *The Collected Poems of Dylan Thomas*. He brought it into the kitchen and set it on the table. Pearl knew which page the poem was on, and as Toby began to read the words, she recited them by heart. " 'Do not go gentle into that good night . . .' "

Toby was beginning to like poetry. Even when he didn't understand all of it, he liked the way the words sounded and the way they seemed to fit together, kind of like a song. He wanted for once to tell Pearl that he understood one of the poems that she picked, but it wouldn't be true. This Dylan guy sounded like trouble. Like he was ready to pick a fight with somebody. All that raging. *Rage, rage against the dying of the light.*

He just didn't know what to think about the poem, so he waited for Pearl to tell him. But she never had, and she didn't now. She acted as if he already knew.

"Shall we check on Blossom?" she said, getting up.

She was smiling the way people smile when they're thinking deep inside themselves.

As Pearl thumped along beside him to the barn, Toby thought how funny it was for a kid to have a friend so old. When she was born television wasn't even invented, or computers, or cell phones. She knew how to milk cows and grow tomatoes and write poetry, things people hardly did anymore. Toby surfed the Web, sent letters through cyberspace, got scanned by magnetic resonance imaging. But none of these differences mattered, they were friends just the same.

As he was riding home, Dylan's words kept singing in his head, even though he didn't much want them to. *Rage, rage against the dying of the light.* How could you keep the light from dying? It didn't make any sense. You could rage all you wanted to, but it would still get dark at the end of the day.

13

Toby's mother oohed and aahed over the tomatoes. She smelled the cilantro, munched on a green bean. She put everything in a bowl and set it on the table. "It's too bad Pearl doesn't have a computer," she said. "You could e-mail her from home."

"She has a telephone," he said.

"I thought she didn't use the telephone."

"She does sometimes," he said. "For certain people." He and Pearl had already worked out a three-ring-hang-up-and-call-again code, so that he could call her any time he wanted to. But his mother didn't need to know that.

He went into his room to check his e-mail.

Hey Tobe what's up? I'm still on the Planet. Guess who's here too? Remember Hula Girl? From Hawaii? She says to say hi. Aloha I mean. She is going to teach me how to speak Da Kine (Hawaiian). Doctor Lattimore is getting married. It's this May-December thing Marcie says which means he's real old and his sweetie is like young. I'm going to be hanging around here awhile. Marcie wants me to read to the little kids because I'm such a good reader she says. Ha. But it will be something to do. Wish you were here. No I don't mean that. Wish I was there. Anyhow I wish we could talk in person. But write, okay? I'll bet you're having the greatest great time. Your friend, Popeye.

Toby went out onto the porch where his mother was thumbing through a magazine. She'd taken off her sandals and set them beside her chair. She looked up. "Want to talk about it?"

"About what?" He plunked down into the chair next to hers.

She frowned her jigsaw-puzzle frown. "I know you're upset. Knowing what's coming doesn't make it any easier, does it?" She sighed. "If I could do it for you, I would. Both of us would."

"Good. Because I'm not going to."

She leaned forward. "It isn't that I don't understand, Toby. I do. I do understand."

"I'm not going back in. You can talk all you want to, but I'm not going to change my mind."

"What's come over you, baby? You were never like this before."

Toby jumped up from his chair. "I'm not a baby! Don't call me that!" He picked up one of her sandals and hurled it out into the garden. Then he felt sort of silly. He stuck his hands in his pockets and went down to the lake. The lake melted through his tears in one big watery blob.

It was after midnight when they finished building the Great Wall. Toby set the last piece right in the middle. His mother sat back. "That was a hard one," she said.

They had worked for hours without saying anything except what had to be said to get the puzzle done. Or his mother would sigh. She sighed a lot. Before his father left this time, he had hugged Toby's mother and she had hugged him back. They'd stood for a long time just like that, with their arms around each other. Watching from his bedroom window, Toby had been too surprised to look away.

"I'm going to bed. I can't believe we stayed up so late," she said. She got up and stretched. "Turn off the lights. And don't stay up, okay?"

"Okay."

Toby waited until he heard the click of her reading

light. Then he got up. He turned off all three lights and felt his way down the dark hallway to his room. When he opened his door, there was Popeye's letter glowing on the screen, still waiting to be answered.

"Dear Popeye," he wrote. Then he erased the "dear" because it sounded too serious, or else too mushy.

Popeye:
DELETE
Hey, Popeye! Guess what? We'll be back in the city on Tuesday. Mom's got this concert she wants to get ready for and
DELETE
Hey, Popeye, the cow I told you about? Well
DELETE

Toby turned off his laptop and the light. Then he went over to his window. He gazed for a while at Mars, spinning alone in deep space. How could he tell Popeye what he was going to do? *Not* going to do. She would never understand. After all she'd been through? Not a chance. Like Mars, she was a warrior. All Toby wanted was to swim out through the stars, away from everything.

14

Toby scowled at the bike's front tire. It was as flat as one of his mother's pancakes. She'd made him eat two before letting him go this morning, and now he couldn't go at all. Not unless he could figure out how to change a tire.

"What's the matter now?" said his mother when Toby slammed back into the house.

"Flat tire."

"Oh. Well. You don't have to go to Pearl's this morning, do you? It's Sunday." She laid her cello in its case and stood up.

"Blossom needs to be milked," he said.

"Every morning?"

"You don't know very much about cows, do you?"

His mother said nothing, but he could tell by her face that she wanted to. "It isn't my fault, Toby."

He knew she didn't mean the tire.

"I know," he said. He wasn't exactly sure why he took things out on his mother, except that she was always so *there*.

"Well, we'd better get the tire fixed," she said.

Toby picked up the phone. Then he checked the back of his hand. "Oh, no!" he said. "Pearl's number was right here."

"On your hand?" his mother said. "You wrote it on your hand?"

Toby shrugged.

"Call Information," she said.

He dialed 411. "Pearl Richardson," he told the operator. Then, remembering Pearl's full name: "Pearl Rhodes Richardson."

His mother's caterpillars jumped. "Pearl Rhodes Richardson?"

Toby dialed Pearl's number, let it ring three times, and hung up. Then he dialed it again.

Pearl answered. "If it isn't you, I'm hanging up right now," she said.

Toby told her about the tire and said he'd get to her house as soon as he could.

"The vet's coming by," she said. "He can milk Blossom." Then came her deep chuckle. "If he remembers how."

"Toby," his mother said when he'd folded the phone. "Do you have any idea who Pearl Rhodes Richardson *is*?"

Toby shrugged. "Sure."

"She's a poet, honey. A very *famous* poet."

"I know," he said. Well, he knew she was a poet. But *famous*?

For his mother, this was even more exciting than Pearl's tomatoes. "Isn't that something? I thought she, well, *people* thought she had died. She hasn't published in years."

"Her light is dying," said Toby, Dylan's words winging back to him. He wasn't sure he wanted Pearl to be famous. He wanted to be the one who knew her best, the one she counted on.

"Her light?"

"She can't write poems anymore because she's going blind," Toby said. "She's been losing her vision little by little, and now it's almost gone." He told his mother what he'd learned about macular degeneration from searching the Web, hoping to find some new thing that could help

Pearl. But it was just as Pearl had said, nothing could be done.

It had taken forever to get his tire fixed. First they had to find the patching kit. His mother surprised him by fixing the tire herself. By then it was lunchtime, and she wouldn't let him go without eating. Even so, he wanted to make the ride to Pearl's last. Who knew how long it would be before he got to ride a bike again? He coasted along, scanning the fields. When he let go of the handlebars, he only wobbled a little before he had to grab them. The ride that used to take forever was nearly over before he knew it.

Why did all the good things fly by so fast while the bad things seemed to hunch down and drag on forever?

And there she was waiting at the fence, just like before. Blossom! Toby kicked himself into high gear, skidding up to Blossom to show off.

"Hey, Blossom," he said, leaning his bike against the fence. "Hey, girl." He threw his arms around her neck. He petted her forehead, where the matted hair grew in every direction. But when he took his hand away, she didn't try to bump it back. "I'll see you later, okay, girl?"

He wondered if you had to have some special magic like Pearl had to understand cows. Or that guy who whispered to horses. "You're okay now, right?" Toby said. Blossom lowed and switched her tail.

He took that for a yes.

Pearl would be so glad to hear that Blossom was her old self again. Maybe she already knew. Maybe when Doc Homann came he gave her some special cow medicine.

Toby found Pearl in the raspberry patch. She was walking slowly down the rows, reaching into the vines and pulling her hand out again and again. Each time, she'd drop whatever it was she found into a tomato juice can. Bugs, probably. Or those fat green worms that were the exact same color as the leaves they fed on. He wondered how she could see them, when he hardly could himself. Lots of practice maybe.

"Guess what?" Toby said, dropping his bike. "Blossom was out at the fence."

"Oh, well, good," said Pearl. "I guess she got tired of lying around the barn."

"She's better," Toby insisted. He took off his helmet and wiped his face with the back of his wrist. "She told me."

Pearl smiled. "She did?"

"Well, not exactly," he said. "But I could tell."

"Just look at all these dad-gummed beetles," said Pearl. She plucked a beetle off a leaf and laid it on her palm, a little black bug with iridescent armor. "Everything has its place, doesn't it? Even Japanese beetles. And its time, too." She dropped it into the can filled with liquid that smelled like gasoline.

It was fun, in a mean sort of way, picking beetles. But it was a hot day and he didn't have his cap. Or any sunscreen. He was glad when Pearl declared that it was time for tea.

Toby made the tea without being asked, lemon for Pearl in the little cup, raspberry for himself in a mug. He set the cups carefully on the table and sat down across from Pearl.

"How come you didn't tell me that you're famous?" he said.

Pearl took a sip of her tea and set the cup carefully in its saucer. She didn't look up, and she didn't answer him.

"You know what my mom said? She said that your public is waiting for you to write some more poems. Like, you have a whole public!"

"My public, eh?" Pearl grumbled. "Well, they'll just have to wait, won't they? I'm not a poet anymore."

"But why, Pearl? You never said why."

Pearl looked up. She worked her mouth a little, which made her jaw wobble. Then she said, "Things got too dark."

"Because you couldn't see?"

"Not that kind of dark," she said. "Life got dark."

Toby waited. He waited for Pearl to find her time and her words, just as she had waited for him.

Then Pearl told him a love story. "When I was just seventeen," she said, "I fell in love with a boy from a neighboring farm, a boy who loved to read as much as I did." Her mouth curled into a little smile. "Reading was a great pleasure in those days. I expect because there was so little time for it. And reading together, why that was simply romantic."

Toby pictured Pearl and a Tom Sawyer kind of guy sitting under an apple tree reading books together. How that could be romantic he just didn't know, though he supposed his mother would.

"We were much too young to marry," said Pearl. "And our parents were simply awful about it. But we were already bound to each other, as surely as tides to the moon."

Geraldine jumped into Toby's lap, settled down, and began cleaning her toes.

"One night," said Pearl, "I awoke to the sound of pebbles tossed against my bedroom window, and when I looked out there was William, carrying a satchel. We ran away to the big city, New York, with only our clothes, a couple of our favorite books, and about five dollars." As Pearl remembered, she stared into her teacup, turning it slowly, round and round in its saucer.

"It was hard, you know. William took whatever jobs

he could find. Factory work mostly. Hard work. But he said I must finish school. I was to be a famous writer someday, he said. Now, isn't that funny?"

When Pearl looked up, her face looked young again.

"Wow, he knew all along," said Toby.

"While he worked I finished high school, then college. And when I began to teach, years later, William signed up for night school. Then, as luck and love would have it, the twins came along. William went back to working three jobs. He was nearly forty by the time he got his law degree. But in no time at all, it seemed, he was a judge. We were all so proud of him. And then—"

All the furrows in Pearl's face seemed to gather, and she was old again.

"What happened?" said Toby, worried that she wouldn't finish the story.

"It all came to an end," said Pearl. "William was robbed and killed. Leaving a flower shop, carrying a bunch of yellow tulips. One of those things that makes no sense. A senseless thing."

"Oh, no!" said Toby, as if the wrong ending had been stuck on the end of a good story.

"After that, the words just wouldn't come. Or I didn't like the ones that did. It was easier just to stop writing, is the truth of it, Toby. A loss of faith, they'll say one day, the folks who'll write my biography. And so I left the city and came back here. It's the house I grew up in."

Pearl's gaze went slowly around the kitchen. She looked to Toby as if she were seeing it all over again, the ancient stove, the worn-out linoleum, the faded drugstore calendar hanging on the wall. "Sometimes it's as if I never left at all."

"Like time travel," said Toby.

"Yes," said Pearl. "Like a wrinkle in time."

15

Pearl handed Toby one of her sweaters. "It can get
cold in the barn," she said. The sweater was the exact
color of pea soup, an old lady's sweater. Toby stuffed it
under his arm.

Blossom wasn't in the barn. She wasn't in any of her
favorite places near the house. "I thought for sure she'd
be back," said Pearl. For the first time, Toby heard worry
in her voice. "She's always home at teatime."

"She's probably still out by the fence," said Toby.

"Give me your arm then," said Pearl, and they began
the long walk out across the field. Stickery burrs clung to

Toby's socks and the legs of Pearl's overalls. They had to watch carefully for gopher holes and dried cow pies that looked like stepping-stones, but weren't. Once, Pearl would have fallen if Toby hadn't had a good hold of her arm.

It was cool for a summer's day. Pearl's long white hair blew around her face until she stopped and tied it in a knot. Then they set off again, Pearl with her walking stick on one side, Toby on the other.

"When Mitchell came with my groceries this morning, he said he had somebody for me."

"Somebody to help you?"

"Yes, a boy from a neighboring farm."

Toby wanted to cry, "But I'm still here!" Instead he said, "That's good."

It was funny how you could be happy for somebody and sad for yourself all at the same time.

"When you come back next summer," she said, "the job will be yours again."

She was old, he was sick. Didn't she think about that? Would there even be a next summer?

They found Blossom not far from the fence, lying in a patch of clover. When she saw them, she flicked her tail.

"These knees can't take much more of this, old girl," said Pearl. Leaning on her stick, she lowered herself and settled beside Blossom. Toby knelt beside Pearl. Blossom's mouth was open, her tongue hanging loose. Her big dark eye rolled. Then she gave a weak low, as if to say she was glad they were there.

Toby shivered, though it wasn't really cold. He put on the old-lady sweater, what did it matter anyway?

There were clouds in the sky, big white puffy ones that were supposed to look like sheep but really didn't.

"Is she all right?" asked Toby. "Why is she just lying here?"

When Blossom lifted her head and bellowed, Toby nearly jumped out of his skin. Then she lowed a couple of times, as if clearing her throat.

"She's tired," Pearl said. "Blossom's had a very hard life this time around."

"She has?" This came as a surprise to Toby. Blossom seemed like a happy cow. But then what did he really know about cows?

"She's grateful I stole her from that old fool."

"You stole Blossom?" Pearl was full of surprises, and this was the biggest surprise of all.

"Well, I had to, you see. She was in very bad shape. Weren't you, girl?"

Blossom took a long, shuddering breath.

"I offered to pay him for her, but he wouldn't let her go." Pearl ran her hand along Blossom's side. "Right here," she said. "Feel this scar?"

Toby felt along the hard raised ridge of skin. "He beat her?"

"Oh, yes. There was something very wrong with that old man."

"So you just took her away from him?"

"Well, we sort of met in the middle. Didn't we, girl?"

Blossom blinked, which Toby took for a yes. She rolled a little, as if to get up. Then she laid her head back down and closed her eyes.

"Some people are born with no heart," said Pearl. "Or at least not one they put to good use. Now you and I, we have our troubles," she said, tapping her chest, "but our hearts are right."

"Didn't the mean guy ever come and take her back?"

"He tried." Pearl chuckled. "It was a regular standoff, let me tell you. Right out of the Old West. Me with my shotgun—"

"Shotgun?"

"He didn't think I'd use it, so I shot it into the air to show him I knew how."

"I heard you shoot it the first time I came," said Toby. "It sounded like an explosion!"

"I shoot it off the first of every month, just to remind him," Pearl said. "He hasn't been back."

Blossom's side heaved, and then she was still again.

"Sometimes you have to do what's right," said Pearl. "Even if it's scary."

"You're a cattle rustler, Pearl," Toby said, just in case she didn't know. "That's a serious thing."

"Oh, yes," Pearl said, with a twinkle in her eye. "A hanging offense."

16

They sat with Blossom for a long time. Now and then Pearl struck up a conversation with the cow, but it was hard for Toby to tell what was going on at Blossom's end. She'd low or throw her head back to scratch her neck against the dry weeds. Once, he thought she rolled her eyes at something Pearl said about a poet she admired. It was surprising how much cows liked a good conversation. The others he'd seen had seemed sort of quiet, maybe even (he didn't like to think it) dumb. But that was just judging a cow by its horns.

Or something like that.

Toby yawned. In the distance he could hear crows cawing, and the drone of a small plane. He looked up. Clouds were moving steadily across the sky, as if they had someplace to go, some other world besides this one. As the sun began to set, a cool breeze rustled the dry grass.

"You need to get on your way," said Pearl. "It will be dark soon."

Toby's chest hurt, as if a hand had squeezed his heart. "Do you think Blossom is d-y-i-n-g?"

"She may be," said Pearl.

"But she's not old," Toby said.

"How about that, girl? Toby says you're not so old."

Pearl's head was cocked to one side, like a bird's, perfectly still, listening. "Blossom really likes you, Toby. Now she likes you more than ever. She says for a middle-aged cow, she's really very old. And besides, being old has very little to do with it."

"Huh?" said Toby. Then, remembering his manners, he said, "I don't get it."

"Well, I'm not certain I do either, Toby. She says it's her time to go, that's all."

"Tell her not to give up!" Toby said, alarmed. "I don't want her to die."

"Did you hear that, Blossom?" said Pearl.

Blossom lowed.

"Well," Pearl said after a while. "She's a very stubborn cow."

Toby pulled his mother's cell phone out of his pocket.

When his mother answered, her voice sounded very far away. "Hello?"

"It's me, Mom," he said. "I'm not coming home yet. I think Blossom's d-y-i-n-g."

"What? Blossom the cow? The cow is what?"

Toby turned away from Blossom and cupped his hand over the phone. "Blossom's *dying*," he hissed into the phone. "I'm going to stay here with Pearl."

"Why is the cow dying? Toby, are you all right? Were you milking a sick cow?"

"I'll call you when . . . I'll call you later, okay? You can come and pick me up."

"Oh, Toby, I don't know . . ."

"I have to stay," he said. The line buzzed and crackled. A ladybug landed on Toby's elbow and began the long journey up his arm. "Mom? Are you there?"

"Yes. Yes, I'm here. Toby?"

"I need to be here, Mom," he said.

Crackle. Silence.

Then came her voice again. "I know," she said.

At first Toby didn't think he'd heard right. "You do?"

"Call me," she said. "I'll be right here," she said. "Right by the phone."

As darkness gathered, the moon began to rise, round and white, through ragged bits of cloud. Pearl buttoned her sweater starting with the wrong button. Then she snuggled down with her head resting on Blossom. She patted the ground beside her. "Blossom is more than happy to keep us warm," she said. Toby settled against Blossom's warm side. His head rose and fell with her breathing.

A wink of a star and then another, and in the middle of it all, Mars, the warrior planet. If only he had his telescope, he could bring the planet close again. He could show Pearl.

But even with a telescope she wouldn't be able to see it. It made Toby sad to think how much Pearl was missing. She couldn't even read the newspaper, and she didn't own a TV. What did she know about Mars anyway? Did she even know you could see the planet with your naked eye?

It was better not to talk about it, even though the whole galaxy was right there shining above them. He would pretend it wasn't there. He was good at pretending things weren't there.

Just like the people who went blank when they saw his bald head. They pretended he was normal. And it always made him so mad.

Toby bit his lip. He crossed his arms over his chest.

"Pearl?"

"Yes, Toby?"

"You can see Mars in the sky now," he said. "Did you know that? I mean, if you could . . ."

"Yes, I'd heard about that on the radio," she said. "I do miss the stars. Tell me what you see, Toby, and I'll see it in my imagination." Pearl lay with her eyes closed, her knobby fingers clasped lightly over her chest.

So Toby told her about the stars, the constellations, about Sirius and Cassiopeia and Orion, about Mars and how he'd seen it that first time with his father. And then he told her that he'd seen his father cry. For the first time ever, as far as Toby knew.

"People will surprise you," said Pearl.

17

Toby was riding Blossom down a crowded street. They were in some kind of parade, moving through crowds of people, all dressed in bright costumes and playing musical instruments. Blossom was covered with ribbons. Garlands of flowers were draped around her neck. A gold crown perching on her head bounced as she trotted along. Blossom was the only cow in the whole parade. In fact, the parade seemed to be for her. She was very happy. He knew that the way you know things in dreams, without having to wonder about it. And she was glad he was with her.

He opened his eyes. All the stars were out now, more

brilliant than he'd ever seen them. Under the dome of the night sky, the stars going infinitely on and on into space, Toby felt himself shrinking. In all of that, what was he, Toby, an eleven-year-old boy? A dot, a speck of dust. Nothing. And then it caught him up again, the way it always did, and he became a part of it, a star or a newly discovered planet, the planet Tobias, there for all eternity.

Pearl was snoring softly beside him. Blossom was snoring, too. Toby started to laugh. He muffled a laugh with the sleeve of the mothball sweater so that he wouldn't wake them up.

The second dream started off being fun. He and Popeye were flying through space, through the stars, holding hands like Peter Pan and Wendy. "See?" said Popeye. "There's nothing to be afraid of."

That was supposed to be his line, Peter Pan's line. But Toby didn't feel like a hero. He *was* afraid. He really didn't know how to fly, and here he was flying. How could that be? You had to believe, said Popeye, that was the trick. If you believed, you could do anything. And suddenly it *was* fine. Like being in water when you knew how to swim.

Then Popeye let go. Just like that. She let go of his hand and went sailing off into space, her arms behind her like jet wings, stars streaming off her fingertips.

Toby sat up, his heart racing.

Pearl was awake. She was sitting up, her hand on

Blossom's side, on a patch of black shaped like Texas. "I think she's going," Pearl said.

"Going?" Toby asked. But he knew.

Toby reached out to pet Blossom the way he always did, but something made him pull back.

"You can touch her, Toby," said Pearl. "There's nothing to be afraid of. Blossom's not afraid."

Toby took a deep breath. He laid his hand on Blossom's side to let her know he was still there. And then, like a whisper disappearing or a door closing quietly in another room, Blossom was no more. His hand felt it, his heart felt it. For a moment, the earth stopped turning and everything was still. It wasn't scary, it wasn't anything he thought it would be. It just was.

"Goodbye, old girl," Pearl said. She smoothed her hand down Blossom's side. Then she put her arm around Toby and gathered him against her.

They sat with Blossom for a long time. There was a stillness all around, in the fields, in the night air. Even the clouds seemed to stop their journey across the sky, and all the crows were silent.

"Blossom was a brave cow," said Pearl at last.

"A warrior," said Toby. "Like Mars."

"Like us," said Pearl. "Like you and me."

18

With Toby's help, Pearl struggled to her feet. "I'm stiff as old shoe leather," she said. "It's time to go in."

Toby looked down at Blossom in her nest of weeds and clover. "But what about Blossom?"

Pearl's smile was sad. "Blossom doesn't need us anymore. I expect she's already gone to wherever she was going next." Pearl and Toby took off their sweaters and laid them over Blossom. Then they began the long walk back over the field. "I wish we had some flowers or something," said Toby.

Their shadows stretched ahead of them in the silvery moonlight. "Do you think Blossom went back to India?"

"It's hard to say," said Pearl. "I don't think she knew. Mostly she talked about clover. Things like that."

"What's there to say about clover?"

Pearl chuckled. "Blossom fancied herself a poet. Clover was a kind of poet's shorthand, a metaphor for all the things she loved. She loved life a great deal, you know."

"Even when the bad things happened?"

"Even then."

They stopped for a rest, listening to the orchestra of night creatures, scurrying, chewing. Singing and dancing for all Toby could tell. It was a world he didn't even know about until now.

"Smell the clover?" said Pearl.

Toby took a deep sniff. It was the best thing he'd ever smelled in his life. He breathed it in until he was light-headed.

"While you were sleeping, Blossom and I had a good long talk, Toby," Pearl said. "She talked about her going, about its being her time to go. Even though she wanted very much to stay here with us, she was ready."

"I wish I'd known her longer," said Toby.

"She could be a real grouch, you know."

"She could?"

"Oh, yes. She had her moods."

They were nearing the house, all its windows dark. Toby listened with ears he never knew he had, saw things as if he had super night vision. He tried to breathe in enough clover to take back with him to the city.

When they got to the door, Pearl put her hand on the knob. Then she turned suddenly to Toby, fixing him with a milky stare, almost as if she were angry. "Blossom said it wasn't your time to go, Toby."

Toby looked at Pearl, at the little old white-haired lady, the famous poet, the crazy witch. "Pearl?"

"Yes, Toby."

"Blossom is . . . Blossom was just a *cow*. I mean, she was a really *cool* cow. But she was just a cow. How could you believe in a cow?"

Pearl smiled, a tired little smile. She reached up and laid a hand on Toby's shoulder. "I believe in you, Toby."

"Pearl?"

"Yes, Toby?"

"Blossom told me something, too, about you. The other day when, um, when I was milking her!"

"She did, did she?"

"Yup. She said that you were going to write a hundred more poems."

"Hmmmph," said Pearl.

19

By late Monday morning, everything was in place. A cow-size hole had been dug in the field, and Blossom lay beside it covered with a flowered tablecloth. "One of her favorites," Pearl said. Toby's mother laughed at that. She didn't understand about Blossom. Doc Homann laid the big shovel of his backhoe next to Blossom and cut the engine. Then he climbed down and picked up his accordion. He was just learning to play it, he said, but he would do his best. Toby's mother raised her bow, and they began to play, the accordion and the cello together, maybe for the first time in history. The song wasn't anything Toby ever heard before, and maybe it wasn't a song at all. The accordion wheezed and screeched, but over it all his mother's cello soared free like an eagle over a chicken yard.

When the song ended, Doc Homann took off his hat and bowed his head, just as if it were a funeral for a person, and not just a cow. So they all bowed their heads while Doc Homann said a short prayer. Toby thought that anybody watching would think they were all crazy. Then all he could think was how perfect everything was, and how beautiful his mother looked with her dark curls and skinny white legs playing the cello in a cow pasture. And when she'd come over and put her arm around his waist, he let it stay. A little thing he could give her.

The bigger thing would have to come later because, for sure, she was going to cry. First in relief, then worry because she'd remember how awful it was for him the last time. So he'd tell her what he'd learned in school about Sparta, how a soldier's mother would tell him to come home with his shield or on it. She was tough as a Spartan mother, and that would make her laugh. Toby was going to fight. He was a warrior after all. He sure wasn't looking forward to it, but maybe the Spartans didn't either.

Pearl picked up her garden shovel and scooped some dirt to sprinkle it over Blossom. Toby did the same. Then

Pearl began to recite a poem she knew by heart. It was about death, which he supposed it had to be, but it sure took death down a peg or two. Toby liked the poem best of all the poems she'd shared with him, even though it had some real old-fashioned language in it. It was like death was real proud of itself and Pearl was telling it right where to get off.

When Doc Homann filled Blossom's grave with the dug-up dirt, Toby, his mother, and Pearl smoothed it over with their hands. They decorated the mound with roses and plenty of clover. Doc Homann pounded the wooden marker into the ground. HERE LIES BLOSSOM, said the marker, COW EXTRAORDINAIRE. Then they all climbed up on the backhoe and rode across the field, Toby scrunched between Doc Homann and his mother, Pearl perched on his mother's lap, her white hair flying. It wasn't exactly a parade, but it was close. What a story he'd have for Popeye.

Afterword

Toby's last visit to the farm was the summer he turned seventeen. The following January, on the morning of her hundredth birthday, Pearl Rhodes Richardson died peacefully in her sleep. In the last years of her life she published three more books of poetry. Her last, dedicated to Tobias Allan Steiner, Warrior, won a Pulitzer Prize. Toby attended the ceremony and accepted the award on her behalf. After graduating with honors from high school, Toby entered Johns Hopkins University and began to prepare himself for a career in medical research. He remains in remission.

Acknowledgments

Like each one of my previous books, this one came into being with the love and encouragement of many friends. I am grateful as always to the Santa Barbara Writers for Children and to Jacob Coffey, as well as to my husband and first editor, Jack Hobbs. A special thank-you to Frances and Janine, whose unfailing support I've come to count on but never take for granted. Julia Cunningham's poetry and great spirit became an inseparable part of Toby's story from the first chapter and always will be. I thank her with all my heart.

Go Fish!

VALERIE HOBBS

What did you want to be when you grew up?
More than anything, I wanted to be a professional ice-skater.

When did you realize you wanted to be a writer?
There wasn't any one moment of realization. It just came over me sneakily, and then I realized that I was one.

What's your first childhood memory?
Sticking my finger into an open light socket. It was almost my last memory!

What's your most embarrassing childhood memory?
Running naked out of the bathroom when the lights went off into the living room full of people. Of course, the lights came right back on and there I was.

What's your favorite childhood memory?
Christmas morning, deep snow, a "real" baby carriage and doll, a miniature piano.

As a young person, who did you look up to most?
Lad: A Dog. I'm serious.

What was your worst subject in school?
Math.

What was your best subject in school?
English.

What was your first job?
Selling lady's underwear at Woolworth's.

How did you celebrate publishing your first book?
I took myself to lunch at an expensive restaurant downtown and had a glass of wine. Then I wrote notes for my next book all over the paper table cover. But I didn't write the book.

Where you do write your books?
In my "office" upstairs, which is also the TV room.

Where do you find inspiration for your writing?
Walking in Elings Park, which has an ocean view and hang gliders.

Which of your characters is most like you?
They are all in some way, but Bronwyn Lewis is the most me.

When you finish a book, who reads it first?
My husband, Jack.

Are you a morning person or a night owl?
Definitely morning.

What's your idea of the best meal ever?
Fresh-caught salmon from the Pacific Northwest, a glass of Jaffurs Syrah, and chocolate mousse for dessert.

Which do you like better: cats or dogs?
Dogs (but please don't tell Molly, my cat).

What do you value most in your friends?
Their ability to listen and to love me unconditionally.

Where do you go for peace and quiet?
My backyard.

What makes you laugh out loud?
My grandkids, Diego (six) and Rafael (two and a half). Just about everything they do cracks me up.

What's your favorite song?
"I Will Survive."

Who is your favorite fictional character?
Dorothea Brooke, *Middlemarch*.

What are you most afraid of?
Poverty.

What time of the year do you like best?
Fall (with Spring a close second).

What is your favorite TV show?
The Office.

If you were stranded on a desert island, who would you want for company?
My husband, Jack.

If you could travel in time, where would you go?
Paris, 1920.

What's the best advice you have ever received about writing?
Write from the heart.

What do you want readers to remember about your books?
We are amazing and powerful human beings, each and every one of us. Sometimes we lose our way but we can always find it again.

What would you do if you ever stopped writing?
Read. Travel. Whine a lot.

What do you like best about yourself?
My sense of humor.

What is your worst habit?
I fall into pessimism and believe that I will never write another book, or a good enough book.

What do you consider to be your greatest accomplishment?
Learning little by little to see the bright side of things.

Where in the world do you feel most at home?
Santa Barbara, California, and Volcano, Hawaii.

What do you wish you could do better?
I wish I could write and illustrate a picture book.

What would your readers be most surprised to learn about you?
I once raced cars.

Keep reading for an excerpt from
Valerie Hobbs's **Lucy in the Sky**,
coming soon in hardcover from
Farrar, Straus and Giroux.

EXCERPT

Lucy sat on the porch steps with her arms hugging her legs and a big black bag over her head.

It wasn't a bag anybody could see. It was the kind you feel when you're in a very deep funk, which is exactly where Lucy was.

She wanted this afternoon, this blazing hot August afternoon, for herself. She wanted to swim. She *needed* to swim.

She needed to spend the day at the pool with Megan, her very-best-in-the-world friend.

She needed not to spend the afternoon making model airplanes with Eddie.

She lifted the edge of the bag and peeked out at the lawn that wasn't. Two weeks ago her father had announced his retirement from lawn care and turned the whole front yard to rocks. Glittery white rocks with dusty green cacti sticking up all over the place like warts on the back of a toad.

"Dogs won't come near this stuff!" he had said, planting the last of the thorny cacti. "Great, huh?"

Lucy had rolled her eyes at her mother, who covered her mouth to keep from cracking up. "Yeah, Dad. *Great!*" A laugh exploded out of her and then her mother was laughing, too, both of them holding their sides and gasping for breath.

"What?" said her father, lifting his hands. "*What?*"

He really didn't get it.

Now Lucy sat staring at the rocks, which glittered back with evil intent.

Her grandmother would not like the new "lawn." She would call it artificial, which is what it was. But Lucy wouldn't have to tell her about it. At Grams', surrounded by pine trees and cool, clean air, she'd probably forget all about the ugly yard. She couldn't wait to be there.

Meanwhile, there was Eddie.

Lucy twisted her friendship bracelet around and around on her wrist. Megan wouldn't have any trouble making this decision. She would get right up and go into her house and announce what she was going to do.

Megan was brave, Lucy was a wimp. That's the way it had always been and that's the way it always would be.

Like this stupid lawn. Permanent.

Wiping sweat from her forehead, Lucy got up. Sweat beneath her nose and behind her knees, sweat rolling down her back. It was just too darned hot.

"Okay," she said aloud. "Okay. That's *it* then. Wimp no more!"

She clenched her teeth for courage and stomped into the house.

"Mom!"

"Don't yell. I'm right here."

Lucy went into the kitchen, where her mother was sitting at the table paying bills. She looked at Lucy over the top of her red-rimmed reading glasses. "I thought you were gone," she said.

"Well, I'm not. I'm not going." Heart clicking like a cricket in her throat.

"To Eddie's? You're not?" Her mother put her pen down. She took off her glasses and laid them on the table.

Lucy went to the sink and filled a glass with water. "It's too hot!"

"And?"

"*And* I'm going to the pool. With Megan." The water in the glass jiggled in her hand.

Lucy's mother blinked. She blinked three more times before she said, "Does Eddie's mother know this?"

Lucy shrugged. "No."

The kitchen got quiet, as if it were listening for what would happen next. Only the refrigerator droned its usual bored hum.

Lucy's mother sighed, a sigh that came up from a place deep within her and tunneled down her nose. "Lucy."

"I know. I know. I'll tell Mrs. Munch."

Waldo got up from his spot beneath the table. Thwacking the table leg with his tail, he begged Lucy for a pat.

"What about Eddie?" said her mother.

"What about him?" Waldo needed a bath. Badly.

"He has special needs. You know that. That's why Mrs. Munch hired you this summer."

Waldo let out a long, contented fart.

"Waldo!" they both said. Waldo cocked his head. What was wrong? Turning three times, he settled himself under the table and closed his eyes.

"Are you going to tell Eddie you're not coming over?" her mother said.

Eddie was thirteen. Until this summer he had been in a special school and Lucy had seen him only twice in her life.

But all that had changed.

Lucy's heart thunked. "His mother can tell him."

Her mother sighed. "I'm sure she can. But Eddie's the one who—"

Lucy looked up at the ceiling, where a spider had built a wispy bridge to the light fixture. She sighed dramatically. "Okay! So I'll tell Eddie."

"It's the least you can—"

"*Okay*, I said." Lucy stomped out the kitchen door and into the carport. What good was being twelve if your mother still ran your life?

She grabbed her bike and pushed it out to the driveway. Pulling her phone out of her pocket, she shot a message to Megan: CU AT POOL.

Swimsuit, towel, sunscreen, water.

She went back inside. Zipping quickly through the kitchen and up the stairs, she grabbed what she needed and left.

Eddie's house was four blocks from Lucy's, a similar two-story structure with drab gray siding. The one big difference, bigger since her father had redone the front yard, was that the Munches had a green lawn full of wooden toys. There were always at least ten of Mrs. Munch's handmade whirligigs sprouting out of the grass like cartoon flowers.

Lucy leaned her bike against Mrs. Munch's battered blue Volvo and went up onto the porch. She knocked on the screen door, which always rattled no matter how lightly you knocked.

The inner door opened and Mrs. Munch, almost as wide as she was tall, appeared behind the screen.

"Hi, Lucy," she said, smiling. "Eddie's been waiting for you."

She pushed open the screen door but Lucy didn't move.

"I, uh. I can't hang out with Eddie today," Lucy said,

her heart hammering. "I have to go somewhere. With my, with my mom."

The lie went immediately to the top of her head and sat there, knitting a headache.

"Oh!" said Mrs. Munch. Her dark eyebrows lifted like wings. "Eddie will be so disappointed. But of course if you have another appointment . . ." Her voice trailed off.

"Yeah, teeth!" said Lucy, tapping her front teeth, as if Mrs. Munch didn't know she had them.

The sun, laughing maniacally, bore down upon her already-pounding head.

Mrs. Munch's eyebrows landed and she smiled her sad smile. "Don't worry, dear. I'll tell him. Shall we expect you Saturday, then?"

"Oh! No! I mean, I can't. That's the day I leave for my grams' house."

"Oh. Oh, dear."

The waiting sat between them like an itch, until Lucy couldn't stand it anymore. "Well, maybe I can come for a little while. You know, to say goodbye and all."

"Yes," said Mrs. Munch, clasping her hands together. "That would be lovely. I'll tell Eddie."

She reached out and pushed the screen wider. "Would you like to come in for a minute? I've got some cold lemonade."

"No, thank you. I've gotta go." Stepping back, Lucy wiped the sweat from beneath her nose with the back of her wrist. Sweat trickled down her spine, seeped out from under her arms. "Well, goodbye, then. My mom's waiting!" Her voice had climbed like a frantic monkey. Anybody but Mrs. Munch, a sweet lady who was sort of out of it, would hear the lie. "See you Saturday!"

She hopped on her bike and fled.

ALSO AVAILABLE
FROM SQUARE FISH BOOKS

Four Unique Stories About Never Giving Up

Lassie Come-Home · Eric Knight
Illustrated by Marguerite Kirmse
ISBN: 978-0-312-37131-9 · $6.99 US / $8.50 Can

The enduring classic story of a young boy
and his devoted companion is a heart-wrenching
and compelling adventure.

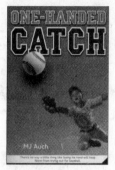

One-Handed Catch · MJ Auch
ISBN: 978-0-312-53575-9 · $6.99 US / $7.99 Can

Not even losing his hand can keep Norm
from trying out for the baseball team.

"Moving and thought-provoking."—*Kirkus Reviews*

Wing Nut · MJ Auch
ISBN: 978-0-312-38420-3 · $6.99 US / $7.99 Can

Sometimes "home" is found where you least expect it.

"A good book for reluctant boy readers."—*Booklist*

Home of the Brave · Katherine Applegate
ISBN: 978-0-312-53563-6 · $6.99 US / $7.99 Can

A beautifully wrought novel about an immigrant's
journey from hardship to hope.

"A memorable inside view of an outsider."
—*Publishers Weekly*

★ "Moving."—*School Library Journal*,
Starred Review

SQUARE FISH
WWW.SQUAREFISHBOOKS.COM
AVAILABLE WHEREVER BOOKS ARE SOLD

RELEASED FROM THE
INVENTORY OF THE
TAMPA-HILLSBOROUGH
COUNTY LIBRARY SYSTEM